The
All New
JONAH
TWIST

Also by the author
INVISIBLE LISSA

The All New Jonah Twist

by Natalie Honeycutt

Bradbury Press ○ New York

Bradbury Press
An Affiliate of Macmillan, Inc.
866 Third Avenue, New York, NY 10022
Collier Macmillan Canada, Inc.
Manufactured in the United States of America
The text of this book is set in 12 pt. Caledonia.
4   6   8   10   9   7   5

Library of Congress Cataloging in Publication Data
Honeycutt, Natalie. The all new Jonah Twist.
Summary: Jonah's efforts to survive the third
grade are complicated by the new boy in class,
who has the potential for either becoming a
friend or beating him up.
[1. Schools—Fiction.   2. Friendship—
Fiction]   I. Title.
PZ7.H7467   1986   [Fic]   85-28048
ISBN 0-02-744840-1

For my mother
with love

O

O

And for my father
Linwood Benjamin Honeycutt
1915–1985
also with love

one

○ IF EQUIPMENT could help you do well in third grade, Jonah Twist was ready. He had a Garfield binder with a Velcro fastener, a plastic zippered pencil pouch, binder paper, a pink eraser with *Acme* printed on one side, and a package of one dozen yellow pencils, No. 2.

Jonah tore open the packet of pencils and poured them out on his bed. Then he shook his head. It'll take more than equipment to do well in third grade, he thought. It'll take a miracle. A flashy one. Like a teacher who is deaf and blind. Or an all new Jonah Twist.

He snapped the rings on his binder a few more times, just to make sure they worked right. They did. Then he scooped up the pencils and went downstairs to sharpen them.

In the kitchen, Jonah's mother was mixing something in a bowl and humming along with a song on the radio. Jonah opened the broom closet where the sharpener hung. He stuck a pencil into the sharpener, positioned it carefully, and started grinding. His mother hummed more loudly.

Mrs. Twist always listened to the radio and hummed while she cooked. She said she hated cooking, and the radio helped to take her mind off it. Jonah thought she'd be a better cook if she paid more attention to what she was doing.

"What are we having for dinner?" he asked.

"Wait and be surprised," she said.

She always said that. But Jonah didn't want to be surprised. If it was going to be something horrible, he wanted to know ahead of time. Jonah left a pencil sticking out of the sharpener and went to look over her arm.

"It looks like barbecue sauce," he said.

"It is," Mrs. Twist said.

That meant chicken. Barbecued chicken. Burnt. Jonah was glad he had looked. He went back and finished the pencil. One down, eleven to go.

While he was working on the fifth pencil, Jonah's brother Todd came in the back door. He was wearing his running clothes and sweating.

"I just ran the mile in four-forty-eight," he said. "I'll be a cinch to get on the cross-country team this year."

"Good for you," Mrs. Twist said.

"But I'll need new shoes," Todd said, waving a foot in the air. "These are shot."

Mrs. Twist turned to look. "They seem fine to me, Todd. Are you sure you can't use them a while longer? Your running shoes are always so expensive."

"But they're important," Todd said. Then he started explaining to his mother about balance and counters and lasts and pressure points, a lot of technical stuff that Jonah didn't understand. The way Jonah had it figured, Todd just liked new shoes.

Finally, Mrs. Twist gave up. "Okay, Todd, we'll buy them as soon as I get my next paycheck. But you'll have to make do until then." She opened the refrigerator and pulled out a package of chicken.

I knew it, Jonah thought.

"I need new shoes, too," he said. He didn't really, but he imagined it was worth a try.

"Jonah," she said, "are you still sharpening those pencils? I thought you'd be done by now."

"Eight down, four to go," Jonah said.

"You let him sharpen a whole dozen pencils?" Todd asked. "The first day of school's tomorrow. At the rate Jonah does things, he'll never make it." Then he laughed.

"Very funny," Jonah said. Todd thought he was so great just because he was in eighth grade. If Jonah ever got to eighth grade, he'd use a pen like Todd did. You don't need to sharpen pens.

Anyhow, Todd probably wouldn't care if all the pencil points came out off-center. Jonah cared.

Once Jonah had seen Todd in front of the bathroom mirror, smiling at himself. "Todd Terrific," he'd said to his face in the mirror.

Todd the Toad, Jonah had said in his mind.

At dinner, Todd used up most of the conversation talking about the classes he would be taking in school this year.

"Algebra will be a snap," he said.

"It should be," Mrs. Twist said. "You've always been good at math."

Jonah pulled the burned skin off his chicken and poked the meat with his fork.

"And Spanish will be easy," Todd went on. "Dad says kids in California just naturally pick up a lot of Spanish."

"*Agua,*" Jonah said, pointing to his mother's water glass. He'd learned that in his own house, on Sonora Street in Westmont, California, watching "Sesame Street" when he was little. He wondered if that was what Todd meant.

"Eat your chicken," Mrs. Twist said, patting his arm.

"And only five other kids besides me get to be in the advanced computer class," Todd continued.

"That's quite an honor!" Mrs. Twist said.

Listening to how great Todd was began to spoil Jonah's appetite. He picked up his corn on the cob and started eating it slowly, in very even rows.

"I'll be learning Pascal this year," Todd said. And he kept talking about computers until Jonah had finished the whole ear of corn. There had been three hundred and thirty-six kernels of corn on the ear, give or take a few. Jonah had counted.

Finally, Mrs. Twist turned to Jonah and asked, "And what are you looking forward to most about third grade, Jonah?"

"Recess," Jonah said. He knew it wasn't what his mother wanted to hear, but it was the only thing that came to mind.

"Jonah," Mrs. Twist said, "there's more to third grade than recess."

"I know," Jonah said, "but that's my favorite part."

Just about the only bad thing about summer vacation was not having anyone to play with. It seemed as though all the kids in Jonah's class lived way on the other side of Mills Elementary School, while most of the kids in Jonah's neighborhood were the kind who still drooled. Every time a new family moved into the neighborhood, Jonah tried to be on hand to see if there was anyone his size. But there never was. If there was anything good to be said about starting third grade, it would be that Jonah would have real eight-year-olds to play with almost daily.

"Well, you'll like third grade," Mrs. Twist said. "You'll have Mrs. Lacey this year, and she's very nice. She was crazy about Todd."

Jonah groaned. He didn't want Mrs. Lacey. And that was just why he didn't want her. Todd's teachers were always "crazy" about him. Then they'd get Jonah, and they'd be crazy about him, too—for about two days. After that, they were just disappointed.

And Jonah knew why. He could list his crimes from memory: Takes too long. Dawdles. Doesn't pay attention. Gets distracted. Forgets to tend to business. Is slow. Slow, slow, slow.

"You're lucky," Todd said. "Third grade is easy. When you get in junior high school, they really make you work hard." He was pushing his food around on his plate and looking proud of how hard he had to work.

Second grade was hard, Jonah remembered. Especially for him. Last year, right after spring vacation, his second-grade teacher had told Kenny Ota he was ready for third-grade work. But she'd never said that to Jonah, not even on the last day of school when she'd told several of his classmates she was sure they'd do well in third grade. When Jonah had said good-bye, she'd just said, "Good luck." Third grade was going to be impossible.

"Eat your chicken," Mrs. Twist prodded again. Jonah looked at his chicken. He wondered if she was going to make him eat the burned skin, too. Todd had eaten all of his. But Jonah noticed that most of Todd's salad was pushed to one side of his plate and covered with a lettuce leaf.

"Todd's hiding all his tomatoes under a lettuce leaf," he said as he picked up his chicken.

"Todd, eat your tomatoes," Mrs. Twist said.

"That's for Woz!" Todd said. Woz was Todd's hamster. He'd named it after some genius who started a computer company. "Woz loves tomatoes, and I'm saving them for him."

"With dressing?" Mrs. Twist asked.

"Sure. *Most* of all with dressing," Todd said. The night before, Jonah recalled, Todd had saved most of his filet of sole for Woz.

Jonah looked at his plate. He eyed the kidney beans his mother had served in his salad. Jonah hated kidney beans. If only he had a pet to feed his beans to. If only he had a pet, *period*.

"I wish I had a pet," Jonah said. He speared a kidney bean.

"Oh, Jonah, I don't want any more pets," his mother said. "A hamster is enough."

"But that's Todd's pet. And anyway, I want a pet for *me*, not for you."

"But I'd end up taking care of it," Mrs. Twist said. "And I already have you and Todd. Three pets is enough."

Jonah knew his mother was being hard to talk to on purpose. Sometimes, when she started being tricky in the middle of a conversation, he would just give up. But he really did want a pet. So he wasn't going to say simply, "Oh, Mom . . ." and forget it.

"We're not pets," he said. "We're kids. And *I'd* take care of my pet, just the way Todd takes care of his hamster. So can I have one?"

Mrs. Twist put her fork down and leaned back in her chair. Her face became serious. "Jonah," she said, "Todd is thirteen years old. And he's very responsible. I don't have to worry about Woz, because Todd takes very good care of him without being reminded. But you . . ."

Uh-oh, Jonah thought. Here we go.

". . . you forget things," his mother said. "I have to remind you of everything at least ten times, and even then you don't get things done on time."

Jonah started to slink down in his chair.

"If you had a pet, *I'd* be responsible for it," she went on. "Frankly, Jonah, I have plenty of responsibilities without adding another."

Jonah slunk even lower in his chair.

"So when you're old enough to be responsible, *then* you can have a pet," Mrs. Twist said. "That's that." She leaned forward and picked up her fork.

Jonah stared at the edge of the table. It didn't seem fair. As far as he could tell, Todd was *born* responsible, while he, Jonah, was not. He tried to be responsible. But somehow he never managed it. Did this mean that he would never have a pet? All because of the way he was born?

Jonah ran his fingernail along the edge of the table. Maybe he just hadn't tried hard enough. Maybe if he put his mind to it, if he tried really, really hard, he could be good and smart and fast like Todd.

"How responsi—" Jonah's voice was weak and croaky. He had to start over. "How responsible would I have to be to have a pet?" he asked.

"Responsible enough," his mother said.

"But how *much?*" Jonah persisted. "What would I have to do? If I remembered to clear my dishes, would that be enough?"

"It's not just dishes," his mother said. "It's

everything. You know—not having to be nagged all the time, doing well in school, that sort of thing. The usual."

Whew. That sounded like a lot to Jonah. He didn't know if he could do that much. But, he thought, he could at least try.

"And if I'm really responsible, I can have a pet?" he asked, checking.

"Yes," his mother said.

Jonah took a deep breath and sat up straight. He took a big bite out of his chicken and chewed as fast as he could. Maybe there was a chance. It would be worth it if there was really a chance.

"What kind of a pet did you have in mind?" his mother asked.

Jonah considered. What he really wanted was a marmot. The marmot was his favorite animal. Every summer since his parents were divorced, their father had taken Jonah and Todd for a three-week camping trip through the Sierra Nevada. And every year Jonah had seen at least one marmot, sometimes more.

The only trouble was that marmots were wild and spent much of the cold High Sierra year hibernating. Where would I keep a marmot in the winter? he wondered. In the refrigerator?

"A snake?" he asked.

"No," Mrs. Twist said. "No snakes. No reptiles of any kind. I couldn't live with a reptile."

It struck Jonah that even being responsible wasn't good enough for some things. Jonah tried to think of a pet his mother would approve of, maybe even like.

"A cat?" he asked.

Mrs. Twist considered. "Yes," she said. "A cat might be nice. I could live with a cat."

"Hey!" Todd said. "Not a cat! Will Watson had a cat, and it jumped on top of his hamster's cage. The hamster keeled over of a heart attack. Dead. A cat could be dangerous for Woz!"

Somehow the idea of Woz lying on his back, his little feet in the air and X's where his eyes should be, didn't make Jonah feel as sad as he thought it should. He looked at Todd and smiled.

two

○ WHEN the steady *beep, beep, beep* of Jonah's alarm clock woke him the next morning, he thought it was a mistake. It was barely light outside, and he couldn't hear the sounds of his mother in the kitchen making coffee. It couldn't be time to get up yet.

Then he remembered. Today was the first day of school. More important, it was the first day of the new Jonah Twist. Starting today, he was going to be the fastest, best, most responsible eight-year-old ever. He had set his clock to get up extra early, so he'd be ready before anyone else.

He put on his green jersey with the white stripes on the sleeves. And he put on his best pair of blue jeans. Then, even though his pants would stay up without them, he put on his belt.

Jonah's shoes squeaked around the kitchen floor as he got a bowl, spoon, and a box of cereal. He was nearly done eating his second bowlful when his mother arrived in the kitchen.

"I was going to cook you something hot this morning," she said. "Looks like I'm too late."

"That's okay," Jonah said. "I like this stuff. Anyhow, I don't want to be late to school."

His mother ran water into the teakettle. "Not much chance of that," she said. "It's only seven-fifteen. We don't need to leave for an hour." She started measuring coffee into a paper cone.

"I'm going to walk by myself," Jonah said. "I want to be early."

"But I'd be happy to drop you at school on my way to work," Mrs. Twist said. "There's plenty of time."

"No, thanks. I'll walk."

His mother leaned over and gave him a squeeze. "I guess you're getting pretty grown up, huh?"

"Yeah," Jonah said. He put down his spoon and drank the rest of the milk in the bottom of his bowl. Then he got up and put his bowl in the sink. Usually he forgot and left it on the table, but the new Jonah didn't forget things.

"As long as you're going to be so grown up, Jonah, maybe you'll make your bed while I pack your lunch."

"Sure thing!" said the All New Jonah Twist.

He not only made his bed but also brushed his teeth, put on his watch, and combed his hair.

Hair combing was a waste of time, as far as Jonah was concerned. In five minutes it would look the way it always looked. But it would make his mother happy.

Todd had just wandered sleepily into the kitchen when Jonah streaked back in, his binder under his arm.

"I even combed my hair," he told his mother, just in case she couldn't tell.

"Good for you," she said.

Jonah picked up his lunch box. "Can I go now?" he asked.

"What's the big idea?" Todd asked. "It's way too early for school."

"Jonah *wants* to be early," their mother explained.

"But he's going to be more than early. He's going to be *first*."

"That's the whole idea," Jonah said. "Can I go, Mom?"

"I suppose so," she said. She walked with him to the front door. "The key is in the usual place. And don't forget to phone me at work as soon as you get home."

"I won't," he said, and kissed her.

"Have a good first day," she called as he ran down the steps.

Jonah waved.

He ran down Sonora Street to the corner. Mr. Rosetti, who lived in the corner house, was in a robe on his front porch, picking up the morning paper. Mr. Rosetti was about seventy years old, and Jonah liked him better than almost anyone on the block. For some long time it had been Jonah's habit to ride across the corner of Mr. Rosetti's lawn on his bike, whenever he was turning onto Manzanita Avenue. Then one day Mr. Rosetti was outside trimming a shrub when Jonah came by. Jonah stuck carefully to the sidewalk as he turned the corner. But Mr. Rosetti hailed him, "Say, young man!"

Jonah stopped, sure that Mr. Rosetti was going to demand to know if Jonah had been riding his bike across the Rosetti lawn.

"Yes, sir?" Jonah said, hoping that good manners might save him from a lecture.

"You'll notice that I haven't planted any trees or shrubs on this part of the lawn," Mr. Rosetti said, gesturing to the corner area.

"Yes, sir," Jonah said.

"There's a reason for that," Mr. Rosetti went on.

"Yes, sir."

"It's because trees and shrubs are a traffic hazard. You wouldn't be able to ride across my lawn if I had plantings there."

"No, sir," Jonah said. He felt he had lost the drift of Mr. Rosetti's conversation.

"And it seems to me that a person loses too much speed if he can't cut the corner," Mr. Rosetti said. "I always cut the corners myself when I was a youngster, and it seems to me the world would be in a sorry state if a boy had to stay on the sidewalk. Don't you agree?"

"Yeah!" Jonah said, forgetting his manners.

"Good," Mr. Rosetti said. "So I'll expect to see you making good use of this thoroughfare in the future. Is that a bargain?" He held out his hand to Jonah.

"It sure is," Jonah had said, giving Mr. Rosetti's speckled hand a firm shake. "It sure is."

After that, Jonah always cut across the corner of Mr. Rosetti's lawn, even if he was only walking slowly. And he and Mr. Rosetti had become good friends. Jonah often stopped to talk with him on the way to or from school, and if Jonah's bike wasn't acting right, Mr. Rosetti always had a tool and knew just how to make the right adjustment.

"Slow down, Jonah," Mr. Rosetti called this morning. "You're early."

"I know," Jonah yelled. "I need to be early from

now on. See you!" He waved and ran on down
Manzanita Avenue.

○ Mills Elementary School was deserted when
Jonah got there. He dropped his binder and lunch
box on the front steps and sat down to catch his
breath. He checked his watch. It was fifteen minutes before eight. School started at eight-thirty.

It was a very long time before anyone arrived,
and then it was Mr. Burns, the custodian.

"Good morning, Jonah," he said. "You're early."

It seemed to Jonah that all anyone was going
to say to him this morning was, "You're early."

"I know," Jonah said, with a little less enthu-
siasm than before.

"Well, sorry I can't let you in," Mr. Burns said,
wiggling his keys in the locks. "No students allowed until the bell rings, you know."

"I know," Jonah said again. He checked his
watch again. Eight o'clock. It shouldn't be too
long now before some other kids got there.

At ten past eight, teachers started arriving. They
glanced at Jonah as they hurried by him up the
steps, but none of them said anything. Jonah wondered when the principal would arrive. He would
have expected the principal to be first, but he still
hadn't seen her.

Finally, at eight-fifteen, two sixth-graders arrived. Then people started coming in bunches. Parents came with little kids, walking slowly and holding their hands as they went down the walk and around the corner toward the back entrance of the school on the ground floor.

Time seemed to slow down. Jonah had noticed that he needed to use the bathroom. He was getting uncomfortable, as well as sick of waiting.

Juliet Fisher, another third-grader, showed up.

"Hi, Jonah," she said.

"Hi," Jonah said. He wasn't about to stand around and talk to Juliet. Of all the girls in the class, Jonah liked her least. The Announcer—that's how he thought of her. Whenever someone did something wrong in class, Juliet would announce it. And most of her announcements seemed to be about Jonah. "Jonah's tipping his chair back," she would say. Or, "Jonah's tardy." Or, "Jonah isn't doing his work."

Jonah liked girls like Sara, who could play ball and minded her own business.

Jonah wished some of the boys would arrive. Like Robbie. He was really looking forward to seeing Robbie.

A boy who looked to be about the age for kindergarten or first grade came and stood at the front steps with the bigger kids. He was wearing camouflage fatigues and a San Francisco Giants T-shirt. Jonah had never seen him before, but then he rarely paid attention to the little kids.

"You have to go around back," Jonah said helpfully. "The kindergarten and first grades are around back."

"Drop dead, you twit," the boy said. "I'm in third grade." He hitched up his pants and turned his back on Jonah.

Oh, great, Jonah thought. A new third-grader, and Jonah had made an enemy of him on the very first day. And now Jonah *really* needed to use the bathroom. He thought the bell would never ring.

"Hi, Jonah."

"Hi, Jonah."

Jesse and Greg had arrived. Jonah was glad to see them. Then Kenny arrived, and then David.

The bell rang. Jonah grabbed his things and joined the crush of children entering the school.

At the door to Room 4, the third-grade room, Mrs. Lacey stood smiling. She was a small, slim woman with broad streaks of gray in her dark hair.

"Welcome," she said as children passed through. "Find a seat. It's nice to have you. Welcome."

The seats were arranged in pairs, three rows with five pairs of desks each. Jonah found a pair of desks in the second row and put his binder down at one place. He put his lunch box at the other place to save it for Robbie. Then he went back out the door.

"I'll be right back," he said to Mrs. Lacey.

"Please hurry," she said.

Jonah hurried down the hall to the boys' room and back. He'd been as quick as possible, but when he got back to Room 4, the door was closed.

Almost everyone was sitting down when Jonah walked in.

"Jonah!" Robbie waved to him from a pair of desks he was sharing with Greg.

"Hey, I saved you a seat . . ." Jonah began. Then he looked toward the seats he had saved.

Jonah's lunch box and binder were shoved together on one of the desks, and someone was already sitting in the other seat. It was the boy in camouflage fatigues.

Jonah hurried toward his desk. There wasn't another pair of empty desks together in the whole room. In fact, there wasn't another empty *seat*. Jonah would have to tell the boy to move. He'd explain about the lunch box, and how he'd saved the seat for his friend, Robbie.

"Good morning, third-graders," Mrs. Lacey said before Jonah had reached his seat.

"Too late," Jonah murmured as he sat down.

three

o JONAH was miserable. The first day of school
had been a complete bust. He still couldn't figure
out how he had managed to be the first one to
school and the last one to class all on the same
day.

And after that, things had only grown worse.
When Mrs. Lacey had called roll and come to
Jonah's name, she'd said, "You must be Todd
Twist's brother. I had Todd several years ago."

"Yes, I am," Jonah had replied. "And I'm just
like him." Jonah hadn't planned to say that. He
knew it wasn't true. Not yet, anyhow. Still, the
new Jonah figured that Mrs. Lacey would be glad
to hear that he and Todd were exactly alike.

But instead, she had just raised an eyebrow and
said, "You are? That's very interesting." She didn't
sound interested one bit.

Then Mrs. Lacey had arranged a "get ac-
quainted" game, which Jonah thought was dumb
because nearly everyone in the class was the same

as last year. Mrs. Lacey said each student should turn to the person in the next seat and find out the person's name and two other things about him. Then she asked each person to tell what he had found out about his neighbor.

Jonah turned to the small, scowling boy next to him and said, "My name is Jonah Twist. I'm going to get a pet. And my favorite animal is a marmot."

"Big wow," the boy said. Then he told Jonah that his name was Granville Jones. "And I could kill you with my bare hands if I felt like it," he said. "Plus I glow in the dark."

"Come on," Jonah said. "I can't say that stuff."

"Say it," Granville threatened. "Anyhow, it's true."

When Mrs. Lacey began calling on people, they mostly said things like, "His name is Jesse Oberly, and he took swimming lessons this summer, and he has a gigantic collection of football cards."

When it was Granville's turn to tell what he had learned about Jonah, he said, "His name is Jonah, and he's going to get a marmot for a pet, if you can believe that." There were several titters of laughter in the room, and Jonah felt himself blushing.

Then it was Jonah's turn. He told Granville's

name, and by the time he got to the part about how Granville glowed in the dark, everyone was howling with laughter and Mrs. Lacey had to call the class to order.

Jonah was sure Mrs. Lacey blamed him for disrupting the class.

To make things worse, Jonah found out that his mother had given him apricot juice in his lunch, and fig bars, both of which he hated. And the only time he got to be with Robbie at all was at recess.

Even that wasn't so great, because they ended up on opposite sides at kickball, and Jonah flied out twice.

After lunch, Mrs. Lacey asked the class to write a paragraph about their summer vacation and what they liked best about it.

Granville hadn't brought a binder, and he leaned over to Jonah. "Give me a piece of paper and a pencil, you twit," he said.

Granville had caught one of Jonah's fly balls at recess, and all together Jonah'd had enough of Granville. He wished he could change his seat. But Mrs. Lacey had said she didn't want anyone to move until she learned all their names.

Jonah looked at Granville and said, "Not a chance."

Granville waved his hand in the air.

"Yes?" Mrs. Lacey asked.

"I don't have any paper or pencil, and no one will lend me any," Granville said.

"Oh," Mrs. Lacey said. "I'm sure Jonah Twist will lend you some, won't you, Jonah?"

Jonah shoved the paper and pencil over to Granville. He hoped the pencil would break right away. But it didn't.

Jonah put his name at the top of the paper. *JONAH EMMET TWIST*, he wrote. He thought Mrs. Lacey would like it better if he put his whole name.

Then, beneath it he wrote: *(J.E.T.)*. Jonah liked having initials that spelled a word. Not like R.W.J. or something. And the new Jonah liked it that his initials spelled a thing as fast as a jet.

Underneath his initials, he started a picture of a jet plane. He gave it two jet engines and folded-back wings. Then he gave it two gunports. And he added a radar dish on top. Then he drew flames coming out of the jet engines. If only he had brought his colored pencils, he could have made the flames orange. He decided he'd bring them tomorrow.

Then Jonah drew a lightning bolt on the fuselage. Right on the tail, in 3-D printing, he wrote: *TWIST*.

24

Then he started his paragraph.

MY VACATION

My dad took me and my brother on a trip. We
went to

"Okay," Mrs. Lacey said, "time's up. Please
pass your papers forward. Make sure your name
is on your paper."

Jonah stared at his paper. He had barely started.
He couldn't hand it in like that. The All New
Jonah Twist wouldn't hand in a paper with only
one-and-a-half sentences on it.

Here he was, slowest again. And on the very
first day.

Jonah raised his hand.

"Yes, Jonah?" Mrs. Lacey said.

"I'm not done," he said softly.

"That's okay," she said. "I'm sure it's fine. Just
hand it in anyway."

"I can't," Jonah said. "That is, I had some
trouble."

Juliet Fisher spoke up. "Jonah's always last,"
she said. "He dawdles."

Mrs. Lacey walked to his seat. "I see," she said,
looking at his paper. "Well, the illustration is very
nice, Jonah. But I'd like to hear the story about

how you went with your dad to see the jet planes. So why don't you take it home to finish it. You can bring it in tomorrow."

Jet planes? Oh, no, she didn't understand. He was going to tell about his camping trip. The jet picture was about his name. He started to say that to Mrs. Lacey, and then he thought that would just make everything worse.

If Mrs. Lacey expected a story about jets, then Jonah had better give her one.

He folded the paper and put it in his binder. Granville, who had written a full page and a half before turning his in, watched.

○ All the way home from school, Jonah had the sensation of being followed. Several times he turned around, but he never saw anyone. Once he thought he saw a pair of camouflage pants disappear behind a tree, but he stood there for several moments and no one appeared. So he supposed it was his imagination.

Jonah knew from experience that if you had a bad day at school you could have a bad imagination on the way home. Once, in second grade, when he'd been in trouble with his teacher all day long, he'd imagined on the way home that his mother and Todd had moved. In his mind he saw his house, empty, with a FOR SALE sign in front of it. He was so convinced it was real that when he got home and found everything as usual, he was startled. . . .

Jonah fished the key out of the flowerpot by the side of the house and let himself in. He wished that someone was home. Even Todd would be welcome company, but Todd usually got home a half hour or more later than Jonah.

Jonah walked upstairs and went into Todd's room. "Wake up, hamster," he said to the pile of wood shavings in the corner of Woz's cage. Woz was sleeping under there, Jonah knew. "Wake up."

The pile of wood shavings moved around a bit, but Woz didn't emerge.

Jonah went downstairs and picked up the phone. He punched the number for his mother's office. He hoped she was there. Some days she was in a meeting, and then he had to leave a message.

"Hi, there," she said brightly. "How's my third-grader?"

He didn't want to tell her that he felt like something run over and left in the road, so he just said, "Okay."

"And how was your first day of school?"

"Harder than I thought it would be," Jonah

27

said. Then, by way of explanation, he added, "I've got homework."

Jonah's mother told him what he could have for a snack, reminded him for the millionth time not to let anyone in except Todd, and told him to call her if he had any problems. Then she said, "And I suggest you get right to your homework. You'll find, with homework, that the sooner you start, the sooner it's done."

Jonah repeated this to himself as he carried his binder to his desk. "The sooner you start, the sooner it's done." His mother had probably meant it to make him feel better, but it didn't work.

He smoothed out his "My Vacation" paper. Then he got out his colored pencils and colored the flames coming out of the engines orange. Then he continued writing.

. . . see some jet planes. They were really neat. They were very big. They were so big they were awesome. And it's very noisy to be around jet planes. SO NOISY YOU WOULDN'T BE-LIEVE IT. You have to plug your ears.

And after that we went camping.

THE END

For a kid who'd never seen a jet plane up close in his life, Jonah thought he'd made it sound fairly realistic. He thought the part about how noisy it was was especially convincing. He could imagine that part without being there.

Todd came home at four o'clock and went straight to his computer. Jonah sat on the floor of his room and worked on a Lego spaceship he had started. He could hear the steady *click, click* of Todd's computer keys and the *squeak* of Woz's exercise wheel, and he felt content for the first time all day.

When Mrs. Twist came home and started dinner, Jonah set the table without being asked. His mother still didn't know that he'd been something less than the model student at school. Tomorrow might be better, he reasoned. And in the meantime, he could still impress his mother by being responsible at home.

Todd did all the talking during dinner, as usual. After all, he had six new teachers to tell about, and Jonah had only one. And Todd and Mrs. Twist already knew about Mrs. Lacey. So Jonah just ate.

At seven-thirty sharp, Mr. Twist telephoned. This was his usual time for calling, on the days he telephoned the boys. He phoned them every third day or so when they weren't at his house.

Since Todd was talking to their mother, Jonah got to the phone first.

Jonah's father asked him how his first day at school had been. Jonah said it was okay.

Then he said, "I might be getting a pet, Dad. Probably. Maybe."

"Great!" Mr. Twist said. "What kind are you getting? A hippopotamus, I hope."

"No," Jonah laughed. "But maybe a cat."

"You should try for a hippopotamus," his father said. "They're great fun to have around the house. I've always wanted one myself."

When it was Todd's turn to talk, Jonah told his mother that his father had always wanted a hippopotamus for a pet.

"I'm not surprised," was all she said. Jonah noticed that she didn't laugh.

four

○ JONAH got up later the next day. The way he saw it, part of his problem on the first day had been in being *too* early. Today he was going to be just a little early, and he would remember to use the bathroom before he left the house.

He pulled on his underwear, socks, and slacks. Then he began looking for his shoes. He found one in the closet, but the other seemed to have disappeared. At last he spotted it, far under his bed. He crawled under the bed on his stomach. It was interesting under there. If you looked up, you could see the slats that held the box springs in place. And through the netting of the box springs, you could just make out the coils of the springs themselves, spiraling upward.

He found a red, translucent piece of Lego on the floor, back in the corner near a leg of the bed. He'd been looking for that piece. It served as a running light on one of his spaceships. He grabbed the shoe and the Lego piece and crawled back out.

31

It took just a second to fasten the running light onto his spaceship. Then it took just a few minutes more to add several antennae to the ship. And only a few more to build a control panel in the sleeping quarters.

"Jonah!" his mother called. "You're going to be late. Hurry up!"

Jonah looked at his clock. Good grief. It was eight o'clock. Where had the time gone?

He pulled on his other shoe, grabbed his binder, and raced down the stairs. He gulped down half a bowl of cereal, said he was stuffed, grabbed his lunch box, and hollered good-bye to his mother as he ran out the door.

Jonah had slowed considerably by the time he reached Mr. Rosetti's house. He had a stitch in his side and was nearly out of breath.

He slowed to a walk. It was all right, he thought. He was probably on time anyway. Just barely.

As he neared the hedge just past the Rosetti house, Jonah thought he saw a small movement. Maybe a dog behind the hedge. He veered off toward the curb as he walked.

"*Hiiyyahhh!*" A small person leaped onto the walk in front of Jonah, his arms flexed in a karate posture. It was a boy wearing camouflage fatigues. Full dress.

Jonah stopped dead in his tracks. It was Granville Jones.

"What . . ." Jonah began.

"*Hiiyyahhh!*" Granville yelled again, kicking a foot toward Jonah. The kick stopped just short of Jonah's chest. Jonah jumped back.

"Cut it out," he said.

"Where've you been?" Granville asked. "I've been waiting forever. We're going to be late."

Jonah couldn't make sense of it. Why was Granville waiting for him? And what was he doing on Manzanita Avenue?

"What are you doing here?" he asked.

"Waiting for you, of course," Granville said.

"But *why?*" Jonah couldn't understand why someone would go out of his way to ambush him on the way to school. Then he remembered what Granville had said—how he could kill Jonah with his bare hands if he felt like it. Jonah took another step back, for safety.

"I live here," Granville said.

"You live *here?*" Jonah looked around. No kids lived on this block. Mostly old people lived here, and young couples who didn't have kids yet. Jonah was sure of that, because it was one of the worst blocks in the neighborhood for trick-or-treating on Halloween.

"Right there," Granville said, pointing to the small, gray stucco house next door to Mr. Rosetti's.

"But some old people live there. . . ."

"Not anymore, stupid. Not since three weeks ago. We just moved in."

Jonah tried to understand this. How could someone have moved in without Jonah's noticing? Three weeks ago . . . oh, Jonah had been camping with his father. Still, it seemed sneaky. And of all the times Jonah had wished a boy his age lived nearby, he had never imagined someone like Granville Jones. He'd never imagined anyone *in particular*, but he was sure that, if he had, it wouldn't have been Granville.

Maybe, if he'd thought about it, he would have imagined someone like Robbie. That would be nice. A regular, normal kid like his friend Robbie.

"Race you to school," Granville said.

"No," Jonah said. "I don't want to race. . . ." But Granville was already off and running.

"You lose!" Granville hollered. Then he was gone in the distance.

Jonah arrived at Mills Elementary just as the bell rang. He had a sinking feeling as he slid into his seat. Nothing had gone wrong yet. At least not that he could tell. He had made it to school on time, and Granville hadn't killed him. Still, he felt as though he'd been through a whole day of school and that everything had gone wrong. He felt like the worst, slowest kid in the class. He felt like he was back in second grade.

Mrs. Lacey called roll. Jonah noticed that she had several kids' names sorted out, but she still stumbled through many of them. He hoped she was a quick learner. He was anxious for her to learn all the names so he'd be able to change seats.

Mrs. Lacey handed out cursive workbooks to everyone. Jonah had been looking forward to starting cursive, especially since he was the only member of his family who couldn't write in cursive yet. Mrs. Lacey demonstrated capital *A* on the blackboard. Down and around, and straight up, then back down. Then she showed them how to make a small *a*.

Jonah carefully started on the first line of his workbook. Down and around, up, then down. Down and around, up, then down. He was careful that his *A*'s touched the top and the bottom lines, as they were supposed to do.

"I'm done," Granville said, flipping his book shut.

Jonah looked at his page. He was one third of the way through. He wrote faster. Down and around up then down. Down and around up then down.

"Is everyone finished?" Mrs. Lacey asked.

"Everyone except Jonah," Juliet Fisher announced. "Jonah isn't done yet."

Jonah felt a tight sensation in his stomach. Everyone was done except him. And thanks to Juliet, everyone *knew* it. He tucked his head and quickly scrawled two more A's.

"All right," Mrs. Lacey said. "Please pass your books forward."

Jonah dashed off two more A's. They weren't nearly as good as his first ones, but he was out of time. He did one more.

Mrs. Lacey was standing beside him. "That's fine, Jonah," she said. "That's very good work. You can just turn it in."

Jonah closed his book and reluctantly passed it forward. He tried to turn his head to look at Mrs. Lacey, but it wouldn't turn. Mrs. Lacey clearly wasn't having any trouble remembering *his* name. But he wished she would. He wished she would forget all about him until he did something better than everyone else. Then she could remember his name. Then it would be okay if she said, "Jonah's finished first, and what wonderful work!" That's what Jonah really wanted.

At morning recess Jonah and Robbie were on the same team. The boys were playing baseball today, and Jonah had been picked second. The rules were that the last person who was picked got to pick the next person. So Jonah had picked Robbie.

When the teams were chosen, Robbie shouted, "First base! I get to play first base."

Jonah yelled, "Right field!" In right field he would get to be near Robbie.

Three of the girls joined the baseball game. Jonah liked it when the girls played, because a couple of them were really good. And also because it meant that they'd be playing "hits and runs" instead of "outs." Everyone on a team would get one turn at bat each inning, and each person could stand there and swing until he or she hit a ball. You couldn't strike out, and there were an unlimited number of regular outs. Then, when everyone on one team had had a turn at bat, the teams switched sides. So the only thing that counted was runs.

Jonah and Robbie joined the line at bat. Kevin was first, and he got to first base. Then Sara batted. On the second swing she hit a grounder and got to second. Kevin got to third. Then Greg was up.

"Watch this," Robbie said. "Greg's a power hitter. We'll have three runs."

"Yeah," Jonah said. "Or at least one or two."

Granville was playing shortstop for the other team. Or he was *supposed* to be playing shortstop, but Jonah had noticed that he was all over the field. Whenever a fielder missed a ball, Granville was right behind him to grab it.

Greg hit a fly ball to right field, but somehow Granville got there in time to catch it. Then, instead of throwing it, Granville made a run toward home plate.

"Geez, he's fast!" Robbie said.

"Yeah," Jonah said, remembering how quickly Granville had disappeared as he'd raced to school that morning.

Granville got to home before Kevin. Then he ran furiously toward third base, caught Sara just as she got there, and tagged her out. Finally he threw the ball to second, but the second baseman missed it, so Greg was safe on second.

Somebody said, "Awesome."

Then Robbie said, "Let's get him on our team next time. He's great."

Jonah had to admit that Granville was pretty good. But he also knew a few things about Granville that Robbie didn't.

"I don't know," Jonah said. "I think he's too dangerous. Anyhow, maybe he can't bat. We need people who can bat."

"Oh, he can bat," Robbie said confidently. "Anyone who can field like that can bat, too. He's nearly ready for the major leagues."

Jonah was in the "next up" place. He reached for the spare bat and started swinging. Jonah knew what he was good at, and he was good at hitting. He'd show Granville a thing or two about baseball.

Jonah stood at home plate. He wiggled around a bit until his feet felt just right, his knees lightly flexed. He touched the bat to the plate, then poised it just above his shoulder. Then he nodded to the pitcher.

The pitch came in fast and Jonah swung. He missed. He glanced at Granville. Granville was shaking his head, a knowing smirk on his face.

Jonah took a deep breath. He shook out his shoulders and got in position again. The second pitch was fast and low. Jonah swung.

Crack. The ball sailed out in left field. Jonah dropped the bat and ran. As he rounded first base toward second, the left fielder was chasing the ball out toward the road. He caught up with it as Jonah touched second base. The fielder threw the ball wildly. No one could catch a throw like that, Jonah thought. He streaked toward third. Suddenly Granville was there with the ball, just inches away as Jonah touched the base.

Granville swore as he reached Jonah. "Get you next time, sucker," he said.

Jonah didn't answer. He just stood panting, one

foot firmly planted on third, squinting into the sun toward Robbie at home plate.

Robbie missed on the first two swings. Then the third went foul.

"Home run, home run!" Jonah yelled. Once in a while Robbie could really smack a good one, and Jonah hoped it would be now.

Robbie swung wide at the next ball.

"Be cool!" Jonah shouted. "Home run!"

Granville danced sideways until he was close to Jonah.

"Real ballplayers don't wear pajamas when they play," he said.

Jonah whirled and looked at him. It figured that Granville would try to get him rattled.

"What do you mean?" Jonah asked.

"Your shirt," Granville said. "I have pajamas just like that, only I don't wear mine to school."

Jonah glanced down at his shirt. It was blue. It was flannel. It had a cartoon of Road Runner on the front. It was his pajama top.

Thwack. Jonah looked up just in time to see Robbie drop his bat and run, and in time to see Granville as he tagged Jonah with the ball.

"You're out, goon," Granville said, and he threw the ball toward first base. Miraculously, the first baseman caught it, and Robbie was out, too.

Jonah doubled up his fist and swung at Granville. Granville hopped out of the way and laughed. Jonah kicked his foot in the dirt, sending up a spray of dirt that fell just short of Granville. Then he walked to home plate.

"Why'd you do that?" Robbie asked.

"Because he stinks," Jonah said. He wished his punch had landed right on Granville's nose.

"But he's littler than you," Robbie said. "And I never saw you try to hit anyone before."

"He's not as little as he pretends," Jonah said. He didn't know how to explain it any better than that. All he knew was that Granville Jones was the smallest giant he had ever seen.

"He's a good ballplayer," Robbie said.

"Who cares?" Jonah said.

o For the rest of the morning, almost the only thing Jonah could think about was how much he hated Granville Jones. And how stupid it was to be wearing a pajama top to school.

Jonah's lunch box contained all things he liked, but he only ate half of them and then slammed the lid shut. His mother could have told him, he thought. She could have said, "You're wearing a pajama top, Jonah." Or, "Where's your shirt, Jonah?" But she hadn't said a word.

Jonah hardly heard Mrs. Lacey when she spoke to him after lunch. "Did you finish your paragraph about summer vacation, Jonah?" she asked.

"What? Oh, that." Jonah opened the Velcro fastener on his binder and pulled out the paper. "It's stupid," he said, handing it to Mrs. Lacey.

"I'm sure it's very nice," she said warmly. "I've hung everyone else's on the bulletin board, and there's a space waiting for yours."

Jonah looked at the neat rows of papers tacked to the bulletin board. Right in the middle there was a space with a small piece of paper with "Jonah" written on it.

Jonah thought the piece of paper should have said: "Jonah is last." He moved his finger over the front of his binder, tracing the outline of the Garfield picture. He liked the tufts of hair near Garfield's ears and the bulging, half-closed eyes.

Mrs. Lacey was talking. She was saying something about habitats. They were going to study habitats this year—habitats of people, and habitats of animals. They would write about habitats for social studies and language arts, and they would report on habitats for science.

"Are you listening, Jonah?" Mrs. Lacey asked.

Jonah's finger was moving around Garfield's toes. He didn't hear Mrs. Lacey.

"He didn't hear you," Juliet said. "He's daydreaming. Jonah does that a lot. He daydreams."

"Jonah?" Mrs. Lacey said.

Jonah heard Juliet's voice in his head, like a tape recording. "He's daydreaming. Jonah does that a lot. . . ."

"I'm listening," Jonah said. He sat up straight.

"Good," Mrs. Lacey said. "Can you tell us what I've been talking about?"

"Habitats?" Jonah guessed. He didn't know how he knew that, but it sounded right.

"Very good," Mrs. Lacey said. "Do you have any questions about the habitat study, Jonah?"

Jonah thought. He had lots of questions. He had all the questions you could think of. He hadn't heard a word Mrs. Lacey said except "habitat."

"No," he answered. He wasn't going to let everyone know that Juliet was right, that he had been daydreaming.

Jonah put his lunch box on the sidewalk and kicked it half the way home. Every once in a while he looked over his shoulder to see if Granville was following him. He didn't see anything.

five

○ As the week wore on, school didn't improve much for Jonah. Sometimes he got work done on time and even did it right. But more often than not he was slow or distracted and finished after everyone else, if he finished at all. So far, Mrs. Lacey had been nice about it. She hadn't even hinted at sending him back to second grade. But Jonah knew that sooner or later she'd get The Look, that look that his second-grade teacher had had every time she'd seen him. It was a look that said: "You're not what I expected; you're not like Todd at all. You're a real disappointment."

The wonder was that Mrs. Lacey didn't have The Look already.

Jonah wasn't having quite as much trouble at home. So far, his mother had needed to remind him to hurry only a few times. But she hadn't yet gotten angry with him. Mrs. Twist had been preoccupied most of the week with a project she was doing at the bank she worked for. Still, she'd never been too preoccupied to lecture Jonah when she felt he needed it. So Jonah thought he was really doing better at home. That cheered him a little.

On Friday afternoon, Jonah dragged his duffel bag out of his closet and started packing. This was to be his weekend with his father, and Jonah liked to be ready in case his father arrived early. He never did, but Jonah thought someday he might.

Jonah put socks, underwear, pajamas, and extra playclothes in the duffel. Then he put in his marble collection, a toy motorcycle that ran on compressed air, and his bear. He zipped the duffel and put it by the front door.

Mr. Twist arrived exactly on time at five-thirty. Jonah kissed his mother good-bye and slung the duffel bag into the back seat of his father's car. Then he climbed in beside it. Todd took the front seat, as always.

Jonah thought that the only bad thing about visiting his father was that he had to share a room with Todd. But one of the best things about visiting his father was that they had bunk beds. Since they both wanted the top bunk, Jonah and Todd took turns. This weekend it was Jonah's turn to be on top.

On Saturday morning, Jonah swung down from

the top bunk in the spare bedroom and went to find his father. He padded down the hall, through the living room, and into the kitchen. Bacon was frying on the stove, and Mr. Twist was mixing pancake batter in a bowl.

"Aha!" Mr. Twist said. "Just in time. I was afraid I was going to have to squeeze the juice myself." He started rolling oranges down the counter toward Jonah. Jonah, laughing, caught them.

He opened the cupboard and reached for the orange squeezer. Then he got a knife from the drawer and began slicing the oranges in half. "Did you ever have a pet, Dad?" Jonah asked.

"Sure," Mr. Twist said. "I had several. I didn't have very good luck with pets, though. First I had a parakeet that died of pneumonia. Then I had a turtle that died of causes unknown. Then I had a goldfish that jumped out of its bowl. And then I had a dog. The dog was a success. It lived for fourteen years."

"Did you take care of it yourself?"

"Oh, yes. Mostly. That's usually the rule, Jonah—the person who the pet belongs to has to take care of it." Mr. Twist poured pancake batter on the griddle and stood watching it as it spread. Then he began to chuckle.

"I was always slightly disappointed in that dog,

46

though," he said. "I had wanted a Great Dane. But my folks said a big dog was too much work. What they got me was a miniature poodle. I liked it well enough until I found out that a big dog eats twice a day and has to be walked twice a day just like a little dog. When I realized I was doing the same amount of work for a smaller dog, I felt rather cheated.

"So take my advice, Jonah," his father said, smiling. "When you get a pet, get the biggest of that kind that they make."

Jonah had put all the orange halves in a long line ready to squeeze, like a factory. "Well, it's probably going to be a cat," he said. "I think cats come mainly in one size."

"I think you're right," his father said.

Todd came into the kitchen in his pajamas, his hair standing up on one side. He reached for a piece of bacon. "Is Jonah talking about a pet again?" he asked. " 'Cause if he is, he's wasting his time. He'll never get one." He bit into the bacon.

"Mom said . . ." Jonah began.

"Mom said you have to be responsible," Todd said. "Knowing you, that's going to be impossible. So I figure Woz is safe."

"Not impossible," Jonah said. "Hard. But not impossible."

"That's the spirit," Mr. Twist said, flipping a

47

pancake. "Anyhow, both of you are going to practice being responsible right after breakfast. We have a tent that needs patching, and a car to wash and wax. So hurry with that juice, huh, Jonah?"

"Yea—" Jonah said, leaning hard on an orange. He loved waxing the car.

"Oh, no," Todd said. "I was hoping we'd go to Santa Cruz or someplace fun."

Mr. Twist poured more batter on the griddle. "Not this weekend," he said. "This weekend is real life."

"Real life" was what Mr. Twist called the weekends when they hung around and did chores. When Jonah's parents were first divorced, Mr. Twist took the boys someplace special every weekend. They went to Marine World, the San Francisco Zoo, Santa Cruz, Morrison Planetarium—a different place each weekend. Then one day when they were on their way to Great America amusement park, Mr. Twist pulled the car to the side of the road.

"This is unnecessary," he said. "You're my kids, not visiting orphans. It's time for some real life." He turned the car around and drove home.

Jonah often liked the "real life" as much as the special trips—sometimes more.

They spent the morning patching the tent and

cleaning the camping gear before putting it in storage. Then they spent most of the afternoon waxing the car. Jonah thought he did a better job than Todd. He didn't leave any streaks of white wax for his father to do over.

When they were finished, Mr. Twist kept walking around the car exclaiming over how good it looked. "Would you look at that," he said. "What a shine! Nobody would believe that car had one hundred thousand miles on it. That's what I call a wax job! You boys are terrific workers."

Jonah was sure that if he could get a pet for car waxing, he'd have one right then.

After they'd put away the cleaning rags, Mr. Twist and Jonah and Todd got in the car and drove to San Jose to get burritos and rent a movie for the evening. Jonah rode in the back seat again.

"So how's school, you guys?" Mr. Twist asked as they headed north on the freeway.

"Great," Todd said. "I made the cross-country team. And I'm working on the greatest program in computer class. You'll see it if you come to Back-to-School Night. Will you come?"

"Of course," Mr. Twist said. "I always do. How about you, Jonah? How's school going?"

"Okay," Jonah said. Just barely, he thought. He'd forgotten all about school since he'd arrived at his father's house, and he didn't want to start remembering now.

"Dad," he asked, "do they have public relations firms for people?" That was Mr. Twist's job—public relations. He worked at a public relations firm in Silicon Valley.

Jonah knew what public relations was about. Mr. Twist had explained it to him. He'd said it was a business for making things seem better than they actually were. He'd said lots of companies needed help to make things seem better than they were and that that was his job.

"Yes," Mr. Twist answered. "As a matter of fact, a lot of people use public relations firms—celebrities and other people who are important. Even the president of the United States has people who help him with public relations."

"He *does?*"

"Sure. The president does a lot of things that would make plenty of people pretty mad if they understood what he was doing. But thanks to public relations, hardly anyone understands anything. They call it presidential politics, but it amounts to the same thing."

For the first time, Jonah thought it might be nice to grow up to be president. "But how about *kids?* Can kids get public relations help?"

Mr. Twist considered his question. "Well, I suppose a child star might. And what's more, he might be able to pay for it. That's the tricky part, Jonah. Public relations costs a great deal of money."

"Rats," Jonah said. He had less than six dollars in his bank.

"Why?" his father asked. "Do you know someone who needs public relations help?"

"Sort of," Jonah replied.

Mr. Twist pulled into the fast lane and passed a beige Honda. "It wouldn't be anyone I know, would it, Jonah? Are you having trouble in school, by any chance?"

Jonah started to say yes, but then he remembered Todd. If Todd blabbed to their mother that Jonah was having trouble in school, he could kiss his pet good-bye.

"No," Jonah lied. "Not me."

"Who then?" his father asked.

Jonah wished he hadn't started the conversation. He was going to try to remember, in the future, that it was sometimes best to let Todd do all the talking.

"Jonah?" his father persisted.

Jonah thought fast. "Just somebody," he said. "Just somebody at school." He thought of Granville. "It's this kid I know, Granville Jones. He's really rotten. He moved in next door to Mr. Rosetti's house, and he's always bugging me."

"Hmmm," Mr. Twist said. "He probably just wants to be friends, Jonah. It's hard to move into a new neighborhood, you know. Most likely he wants to get your attention so you can be friends. You should try to be nice to him."

"Not this kid," Jonah said. "He doesn't want to be friends. He wants to kill me. Every morning he jumps out at me from behind a bush or tree, and he does these karate moves."

"I see . . ." his father said.

"And he told me yesterday he has a black belt in karate," Jonah said.

"Ah."

"And he pokes me in class," Jonah said, remembering an incident during math time on Friday. He didn't mention that Granville always got his work done before Jonah did or that he claimed to glow in the dark. He didn't know what his father would make of those facts.

"Well, I'm not sure public relations is exactly what this boy needs," his father said. "Maybe what he needs is to pick on someone his own size."

"He can't," Jonah said weakly. "There isn't anyone his size. He's the smallest kid I ever saw in my life. And the fastest. And he always wears camouflage clothes, so sometimes he's hard to see."

Mr. Twist started to chuckle, which annoyed Jonah. It was obvious that he didn't understand what a menace Granville really was.

"Hey," Todd said, "I think I've seen that kid. He has a sister who's in my grade. She's small, too. But she's nice. And she's shy. Smart, too, I think—she's in my fast-track algebra class."

"If she's nice, she can't be related to Granville," Jonah said. Nobody nice could possibly be related to Granville Jones. Granville was the meanest kid in the world. In fact, when Jonah thought about it, Granville was probably the reason Jonah wasn't doing better in school. After all, he *was* doing better at home.

No doubt about it—Granville Jones was some kind of jinx.

six

○ JONAH'S mother handed him two dollars as he was leaving the house late Sunday afternoon. His duffel bag still sat in the hall where he had dropped it on returning home from his father's.

"Please stop by the Day Lite Market after you've talked to Mr. Rosetti and get me a loaf of bread," she said.

"Okay."

"You won't forget, will you?"

"No," Jonah said. He was pleased that his mother had asked him to get the bread. Usually she sent Todd.

He got on his bike and pedaled up the street toward Mr. Rosetti's house. Mr. Rosetti had telephoned over the weekend and asked for Jonah to come by. He'd said he wanted to hire Jonah for a small job.

Jonah thought he had caught an expression of pride on his mother's face. After all, you had to be pretty responsible to be hired for a job, even if it was a small job.

54

Jonah leaned his bike against Mr. Rosetti's steps and pushed the doorbell.

"Glad you could come, Jonah," Mr. Rosetti said as he stepped outside. "The job's out back. I'll lead you to it." He walked with Jonah up the drive past the side of his house to the backyard.

"I'm going to visit my sister in Portland for a few days," he explained, "and I hate to leave my garden untended when the weather is so hot. I need someone I can depend on to water the vegetables." He slipped open the latch to the back gate.

"You can see," he gestured. "It would be a tragedy to have all those tomatoes shrivel up just when they're all getting ripe."

"It sure would," Jonah agreed. Mr. Rosetti's backyard looked like the produce section of the grocery store—except that everything was growing out of the ground or on a vine, instead of sitting on a shelf.

Some of the things Jonah recognized, like the tomatoes and lettuce and beans. And others Mr. Rosetti had to point out to him, like the radishes, which didn't look like much until you pulled them out of the ground. Mr. Rosetti pulled one out, rinsed it under the hose, and handed it to Jonah. Jonah didn't ordinarily like radishes, but that one sure tasted good.

Mr. Rosetti explained to Jonah how much to water each thing. The lettuce could take a good deal of water, and it didn't matter if the leaves got wet. But the tomatoes needed just so much, and their leaves should stay dry.

"And don't water the pumpkins at all," Mr. Rosetti said. "They've finished growing, and they're just going to sit there and get ripe." Mr. Rosetti had two of the biggest, fattest pumpkins Jonah had ever seen, smack in the middle of the garden.

"Wow," Jonah said. "Are you going to *eat* those?"

"No," Mr. Rosetti said, "I'm not. As a matter of fact, I was counting on giving one to you. I thought that if you would take this job, I'd pay you off in pumpkin, so to speak."

"That would be great!" Jonah said. Every year, Jonah's father took the boys over to Half Moon Bay to pick out a pumpkin at the pumpkin festival. But Todd had lost interest in pumpkins lately, and Jonah's father complained more every year about the crawling traffic on the Half Moon Bay road.

If Jonah got paid in pumpkin, his father would be happy. And Jonah would have the biggest pumpkin in the neighborhood.

"It's a deal," Jonah said. He stuck out his hand, remembering the first time he had met Mr. Rosetti. Mr. Rosetti gave it a firm shake.

"You've got new next-door neighbors," Jonah said as they walked back to the front of the house. "Did you notice?"

"I sure did," Mr. Rosetti said. "The Newmans suddenly got it into their heads to pack up and leave. They sold the house and moved to a place down the peninsula. A retirement community. Century Village or some such place.

"You couldn't get me to do that. I like having young people around. I like having *old* people around, too, when it comes to that. I guess you could say I like a mixture."

"Like your garden," Jonah observed.

"Yes. Like my garden."

"Did you meet Granville yet? He's in my class at school."

"No," Mr. Rosetti said. "I don't believe I did. I met one boy, though. A little fellow. Maybe five or six years old."

"That's Granville," Jonah said. "He's mean."

Mr. Rosetti laughed. "He doesn't look big enough to be mean, Jonah."

"He manages," Jonah said.

"Then I hope he doesn't hurt himself. It's risky

to be mean if you're small. I will say he has an unusual idea of fashion, though, wearing those military clothes."

"That's so people can't see him," Jonah explained.

"Well, his sister seems just the opposite. You'd have to say she was a quiet dresser. That happens in families, sometimes; kids seem to decide to be opposites."

"Or they just *are* opposites," Jonah said, thinking of himself and Todd.

Jonah hoped that Granville wouldn't leap out from behind a bush at Mr. Rosetti someday. It wouldn't be good to scare someone so old. Especially not his good friend, Mr. Rosetti.

He bumped his bike across Mr. Rosetti's lawn and pedaled down Manzanita Avenue toward the Day Lite Market. He hadn't forgotten the bread. His mother would be pleased. And she'd be proud of him for having a job and earning a pumpkin.

Jonah got the loaf of whole wheat bread and handed the man at the counter the two dollars. He got a grunt from the man and a handful of change.

Jonah counted the change. Twenty-five, fifty, seventy-five, eighty, one, two, three. Eighty-three cents in change. That was right. He crammed it

58

far down in his pants and started home, the bread swinging in its plastic wrapper from his hand on the handlebar.

As he headed back up Manzanita Avenue, Jonah started to pick up speed. He was going to cut Mr. Rosetti's corner fast. He might set a new speed record. He stood and pedaled harder.

"*Hiiyyahhh!*" Granville swung down from the branch of an overhanging tree, landing almost directly in front of Jonah on the sidewalk.

Jonah swerved to avoid hitting Granville and careened into the hedge at the border of the Jones property. He flew off the bike and went rolling, side over side, the bread still in his hand.

"Ha-ha. Got you!" Granville laughed.

Jonah stood up and brushed himself off. He wasn't hurt, but he was plenty mad.

"I should have run over you," he yelled. "Next time I *will*. And I hope I squash you flat!"

"Like your bread, right?" Granville laughed.

Jonah looked at the loaf of bread. It was mashed. His mother would be furious.

He dropped the bread and took off at a run after Granville. "I'm going to get you!" he hollered. "And I'm going to punch your lights out, too!"

But Granville was too fast. In a flash he had

disappeared down the block and around the corner. By the time Jonah got there, Granville was nowhere in sight.

Jonah walked back and picked up the bread. He squeezed it this way and that, and soon it began to take on something of its former shape. He picked up his bike and walked it home.

"What happened to you?" his mother asked as he came in the door. "Your arm's scraped. Did you have an accident?"

"Granville Jones happened to me," Jonah said in disgust. "And he happened to your bread, too." He put the bread on the kitchen counter and fished the change out of his pocket. Eighty-three cents. It was still there. That was lucky.

"His sister may be nice," Jonah said, "but Granville's not. People in families aren't always the same, you know."

"Hmmm . . ." was all Mrs. Twist said. But she didn't get mad.

Jonah went into the bathroom and ran his scraped arm under cold water. In his mind he kept seeing Granville swing down from the tree. It kept making him mad.

Then he remembered something else. A very fleeting expression of fear on Granville's face as Jonah had started to chase him down the street.

60

Jonah wondered if it was possible that a tiny piece of Granville was afraid of him. He *should* be afraid, Jonah thought. Granville might know karate, but Jonah was nearly twice his size. If Jonah ever got karate lessons, he could cream Granville.

That thought made Jonah feel a little better. And that's when he noticed that his arm hurt. He turned off the water, dried his arm on a towel, and went to find his mother. He wanted to tell her about the pumpkin payment.

seven

○ At morning recess time on Monday, Jonah hung back as the other kids filed out the door. All Sunday night, and all through math time this morning, he had been thinking about what he would do. The time had come to get his seat changed.

He approached Mrs. Lacey as she stood erasing the math lesson from the board.

"Mrs. Lacey?" he asked.

She turned around. "Yes, Jonah?"

"Have you learned everyone's name yet?"

"Why, yes." She smiled. "I believe I have. I certainly know yours. You're Jonah Twist, and you're just like your brother Todd—or so you said."

Jonah blushed. He wished she hadn't remembered that. "I'm not really," he said softly.

"I know that," Mrs. Lacey said. Then she put her hand on his shoulder. "What can I do for you, Jonah?"

"Well, I wondered if you had learned all the names yet. Because you said we could change seats after you knew our names."

"Oh, I see. . . ."

"And I need to change my seat. I really do. I want to sit next to Robbie. But mostly I *don't* want to sit next to Granville. I can't sit next to him."

"Oh?"

"It's because he bugs me. And I can't get my work done. And he hates me, besides. He hates me a whole lot." Jonah felt out of breath, even though he hadn't been running.

There were several seconds of silence, and Mrs. Lacey seemed to be thinking. Jonah stood with his chest heaving, waiting for her to speak.

"Jonah, it's very hard to be new at a school," she said at last.

"Yeah," Jonah agreed. Especially if you're Granville and you're mean, he thought.

"And I'd hate to make Granville unhappy by making him feel that someone didn't like him," she went on.

"It wouldn't make him unhappy," Jonah said quickly. "*He* hates *me,* so it wouldn't make him unhappy at all."

"But Granville hasn't asked to have his seat

changed—you have. And, Jonah, if I were asked to place a bet, I'd bet that Granville really likes you. Even though he bugs you, as you say."

"But . . ."

"You see, some children don't know how to show people that they like them. So they pester the people they like. I suspect that Granville is one of those people."

"He's not," Jonah said firmly. "He hates me, and that's that."

Mrs. Lacey gave a small sigh. Jonah felt a little tingling at the back of his neck; his mother often sighed right before she ran out of patience. He hoped Mrs. Lacey wasn't going to get mad.

"I'll tell you what," she said. "If you'll give it two more weeks, and if you'll try to be friendly to Granville, and if things *still* don't improve, then come to me. I'll move your seat. Does that sound fair?"

Jonah considered. He didn't think he could last for two more weeks next to Granville. On the other hand, he didn't want Mrs. Lacey to think he, Jonah, was the one who was mean. He supposed he would have to stay put for the time being.

"Okay," he said. "But if he still hates me in two weeks, you'll really move my seat, right?"

"Right," Mrs. Lacey said. "To any place you like."

"Good," Jonah said. He would *like* to sit next to Robbie.

As Jonah reached the classroom door, Mrs. Lacey called after him. "Jonah, one more thing. Try not to worry so much about your schoolwork. You're doing fine."

Jonah walked onto the playground feeling dazed. Mrs. Lacey thought that Granville liked him, when just the opposite was true. And she didn't want Jonah to worry about his schoolwork, even though she had already figured out he wasn't like Todd.

Mrs. Lacey was a nice teacher—Jonah was sure of that. But she had things all backward about Granville. And she didn't understand about his schoolwork. Jonah knew that if he didn't worry about it, he wouldn't get *anything* done. Then he could forget about getting a pet. And he'd be sent back to second grade for sure. He didn't know how Mrs. Lacey could be so nice and still not understand these things. He picked up a pebble and heaved it in the direction of the road.

At lunchtime, Jonah gave Robbie half of his orange. "I'm getting my seat moved in two weeks," he said. "I'll get to sit next to you."

"Cool," Robbie said. But the way he said it,

Jonah had the idea that it didn't matter to Robbie who he sat next to. It mattered to Jonah, though. He sucked on a section of orange and thought about how glad he was going to be when the two weeks were up.

Early in the afternoon, Mrs. Lacey led the whole class, single file, to the library. Everyone was to look for a book about an animal for the habitat study.

Jonah knew just what book he was going to get: a book about marmots.

Mrs. Lacey said that anyone who didn't know how to find a book was to ask her or Ms. Garrett, the librarian, for help. Several kids went for help right away.

Jonah knew he didn't need help. In second grade, Juliet had been in his library group, and he knew that whenever they were supposed to find a particular kind of book, the quickest way was to just follow Juliet. That's what he did.

Juliet headed directly for a low shelf near the windows, and Jonah was right behind her. Juliet ran her finger along the bindings of several books, then pulled out a big book about horses. Other kids arrived and squeezed in next to Jonah.

Jonah looked at the titles of the books. He saw books about canaries and parakeets and several about farm animals, but he didn't see any about marmots. He moved down a little farther. He found a book about gerbils, and then one about hamsters. Todd had a hamster book, Jonah knew, but he didn't have this one. Jonah pulled it off the shelf.

Almost all the pictures looked like Woz. Jonah turned the pages until he came to a picture of hamster babies. They looked pretty disgusting, with no hair and bodies like misshapen stumps. Jonah wondered if Todd knew hamsters started out so ugly. If he did, maybe he wouldn't think Woz was so great.

He turned a few more pages. He got to a chapter entitled: "How to Feed Your Hamster."

"Your hamster will thrive on a diet of hamster pellets from your local pet store," it said. Then it said that sometimes you should give your hamster crisp green vegetables. Next it told how a hamster saves some food in its cheeks. Jonah thought about how marmots didn't need to eat at all for all the months they were hibernating. It seemed to him that hamsters had a few things to learn.

Then, right below the paragraph about providing fresh water for your hamster, Jonah read: "Hamsters don't eat table scraps, so don't feed any to yours. Table scraps will foul his cage, and they might make him sick."

Jonah was stunned. Either Woz was a very unusual hamster, or Todd had made a mistake. He read the paragraph again. It was clear: Hamsters didn't eat table scraps. That meant they didn't eat tomatoes with dressing, or egg salad, or filet of sole, or any of a long list of foods that Todd regularly set aside for him.

Jonah reached for a second book about hamsters. It was just like Todd's. It had a list of the foods you should feed your hamster, and nowhere on the list did it mention tomatoes or eggs. Or filet of sole. Or large-curd cottage cheese. Or anything like that.

Jonah put the second book back on the shelf and took the first toward the checkout desk and got in line. This was important information. Todd should read this stuff. Maybe there was something wrong with Woz. Or, if there wasn't, Todd could make Woz sick by feeding him table scraps. Or . . . a third thought occurred to Jonah. Maybe Todd just pretended to feed that junk to Woz.

Jonah wrote his name on the card, and Ms. Garrett stamped the due date in the book.

"A nice choice," she said. "I used to have a hamster myself."

"Oh, but I'm going to get a different book," Jonah started to explain. He didn't have his marmot book yet.

"All right," he heard Mrs. Lacey say. "Most of

you have books. So would those of you who have books follow me back to the classroom? Anyone who isn't quite finished may remain a few minutes longer."

Jonah dashed back toward the shelves. He didn't want to leave with the wrong book.

Juliet brushed past him. "You have a book, Jonah," she announced loudly. "You're supposed to go back to class."

"I know, but . . ."

"Mrs. Lacey *said* so," Juliet said even louder.

Jonah glanced around. People were looking at him. His shoulders drooped as he reluctantly joined the group lined up at the door.

Back in his seat in Room 4, Granville leaned toward Jonah and said, "Hamsters, huh? Hamsters are dumb."

"You're telling me," Jonah muttered.

"So why are you doing them?" Granville asked.

"None of your business," Jonah said. He certainly wasn't going to explain to Granville that the hamster book was a mistake.

"Well, I'm doing chameleons," Granville said. "They're just like me. They can camouflage themselves."

"You should have picked glowworms," Jonah said.

"Why?"

"Because they're like you, too. Since you glow in the dark."

"Goon," Granville said. "I don't glow that *often*. But I can be camouflaged all the time. Anyhow, I had a chameleon once. He used to change colors all the time in his terrarium, and he was really hard to find. Then one day he changed colors and disappeared completely."

Jonah thought about Granville in his camouflage fatigues. In his mind he got a picture of Granville disappearing into a bush and never coming back. Jonah felt the corners of his mouth twitch up.

"That's neat," Jonah said.

Granville gave him a level look. Then he reached over and shoved the hamster book onto the floor.

eight

○ ONE THING was sure, Jonah thought as he put his binder and the hamster book on his desk at home that afternoon: nothing much had changed. He was still the Same Old Jonah Twist. He still forgot to pay attention to the important things in school, and he still didn't get his work done.

Now he was going to end up doing a stupid habitat study on hamsters. Either that or he would have to tell Mrs. Lacey he'd gotten the wrong book.

Jonah couldn't decide which was worse.

He phoned his mother at her office, then went down the street to Mr. Rosetti's house. He watered the beans, then started on the lettuce.

At least Mr. Rosetti would be happy when he got back on Wednesday. All of his vegetables looked better than ever, Jonah thought. Even if he did say so himself.

He waved the spray from the hose back and forth over the lettuce. He looked at the huge, orange pumpkins, bright in the afternoon sun. He wondered if Granville ever looked over the back fence and saw them. Granville would probably wish he could have one.

Jonah waved the hose back and forth faster. He was glad Mr. Rosetti had given him this job. He was going to have the best pumpkin in the neighborhood. Maybe in the whole world.

He thought about Mrs. Lacey and what she had said about being friendly to Granville. How could you be friendly to someone who hated you and was always jumping out at you from hiding places? Right after school today, Granville had ambushed Jonah just outside the playing field. Jonah wished Mrs. Lacey had seen that. Then maybe she'd understand that Granville didn't want to be friends. She wouldn't think Granville was so great then.

Jonah froze. That was it. He had to find a way to show Mrs. Lacey that Granville wasn't so great. Then she'd believe what Jonah had told her. And Jonah had an idea—an idea that would get Granville in trouble in school. And what was more, it would seem like Jonah was only trying to be friendly.

He set the hose down, the water running by the roots of the tomato plants, and ran toward home.

"You're a genius, Jonah," he said out loud.

He dumped the contents of his bank on his bed and grabbed a dollar. A dollar should do it. He grabbed an extra dollar just in case. Then he ran all the way to the Day Lite Market.

There were so many kinds of gum that Jonah had trouble choosing. He rejected all the sugarless brands. His parents never allowed Jonah or Todd to chew any gum except the sugarless kind, but everyone knew that the ones with sugar tasted better.

This was a special occasion, Jonah reasoned. Only the best gum would do. He settled on a huge pack of bubble gum. The kind with sugar. The mere thought of it made Jonah's mouth water.

He paid the man behind the counter, got fifty-two cents in change, and ran all the way home.

Jonah pulled open his dresser drawer and hauled out a fresh pair of jeans. He stuffed the gum into a pocket, folded the jeans, and laid them on top of the dresser. Then he put a fresh shirt on top of the jeans. Then underwear and socks on top of that.

There. He was all ready for school tomorrow. The gum was safe where he wouldn't forget it, and where his mother wouldn't see it.

"What are you up to?" Todd asked from the doorway.

Jonah jumped. "Nothing," he said.

"I'll bet," Todd said. "If you're not doing anything, then why is your money spread all over your bed? And why do you look so guilty? Did you buy caps again, Jonah? Mom won't like it."

Caps? He was practically a baby when he bought those caps and exploded them with a hammer on the bathroom floor. That was all the way back in first grade. Did Todd think he was a baby still?

"I didn't buy any caps," Jonah said. Then he added, "And I don't look guilty either. So leave me alone."

Todd shrugged. "Suit yourself," he said, and left.

Jonah rushed into the bathroom and studied his face in the mirror. It didn't look guilty, exactly. Or at least he didn't think it did. But maybe it did look a little odd.

Jonah tugged at his cheeks, then wiggled his eyebrows. He'd have to be careful around Mom. She might guess about the gum. He gathered up his money and replaced the bank on his desk.

At the dinner table that night, Jonah used his best manners, so as not to call attention to himself. They were having ravioli and fresh, raw broccoli. Jonah speared his broccoli with his fork, even though his mother picked hers up with her fingers. Every now and then he wiggled his eyebrows, just so his face wouldn't get set in an odd expression.

"Jonah, is something wrong with you?" his mother asked.

"No. Why?" Jonah was aware he had spoken a trifle too loudly.

"You seem troubled," Mrs. Twist said. "And you've developed a tic around the forehead."

Todd spoke through a mouthful of broccoli. "I think he's up to something. He's been acting funny all afternoon."

Jonah stuffed a forkful of ravioli into his own mouth. "I have not," he said. Ravioli made a good muffler.

"Jonah?" his mother persisted.

Jonah shot an angry look at Todd. Then he noticed the ravioli shoved to one side of Todd's plate.

"Todd's not eating his ravioli," Jonah said.

"I'm saving it for Woz," Todd said quickly. "Woz loves it, and it has even more protein than eggs."

Suddenly Jonah felt sure that Woz wasn't an unusual hamster at all. He was just like all the other hamsters. That meant Woz didn't eat ravioli. What's more, Jonah was sure Todd knew it.

"Hamsters don't eat ravioli," Jonah announced. "And I can prove it!" He shoved his chair back from the table and ran for the hamster book in his room.

He put it down in front of his mother and opened the book to the page that began: "How to Feed Your Hamster."

"There," he said, pointing to the part where it said hamsters don't eat table scraps.

" '. . . don't eat table scraps,' " his mother read out loud. "Hmmm. '. . . will foul his cage.' Hmmm."

A pink color was creeping up the sides of Todd's neck.

"That means ravioli," Jonah explained. "And it means eggs, noodles, fish, and tomatoes with dressing."

Tomatoes. Holy cow, tomatoes! Jonah had left the water running on the tomatoes in Mr. Rosetti's yard.

"Jonah," his mother called as he bolted for the front door.

"Be right back," he hollered.

Before Jonah even got to Mr. Rosetti's house he could see the water. It was streaming down Mr. Rosetti's driveway, across the sidewalk, into the gutter, and down to the storm sewer at the dip in the road.

Jonah wrenched the spigot shut and stood looking around him in dismay. The tomato plants were awash in water, as were the radishes, lettuce, and much of the rest of the yard.

Jonah rushed to where the pumpkins sat. They were still dry. Not that it matters much, Jonah thought. Mr. Rosetti will never give me a pumpkin, now that I've turned his yard into a swamp.

Jonah walked slowly home, feeling numb. In the dining room he leaned against the back of his chair and told his mother what had happened.

"That figures," Todd said. "Leave it to Jonah to drown Mr. Rosetti's yard. And he thinks he's responsible enough to have a pet. Ha! Imagine what he'd do to a pet."

Jonah felt a stinging in his eyes, like tears were coming.

"When it comes to being responsible," Mrs. Twist said, "I don't think you have anything to brag about, Todd. This nonsense about Woz's diet is pretty irresponsible."

"That's different," Todd said. "That's more like a lie."

"My point exactly," their mother said, and rose to carry her plate to the kitchen.

When Jonah's dad phoned that night, Jonah asked him what he thought would happen to Mr. Rosetti's vegetables.

"That depends on how wet they got," Mr. Twist said.

"Pretty wet," Jonah said. "Everything got soaked, and the tomato patch looked like earth soup."

"Well, the lettuce will probably be fine," his father said. "And radishes are sturdy. But the tomatoes will likely burst."

Jonah moaned. Mr. Rosetti would be really upset about his tomatoes.

"I'm looking forward to seeing you next weekend, kiddo," Mr. Twist said.

"Me, too," Jonah said.

Right now, next weekend seemed like the only thing Jonah did have to look forward to. No pumpkin. No pet. And somehow even knowing that Todd would have to eat all his dinner in the future didn't cheer Jonah up.

That night Jonah had a dream in which Mr. Rosetti gave Jonah's pumpkin to Granville. Granville carried it home in one hand, raised over his head—even though in the dream the pumpkin was three times as big as Granville.

nine

○ THE PACKET of gum in Jonah's pocket rubbed against his leg all the way to school. Jonah liked being reminded that it was there. It made him think of the trap he had set, and how Mrs. Lacey was going to find out all about Granville. That pack of gum, he thought, was like a loaded weapon.

In his seat at eight-thirty, Jonah knew Granville was late for school.

By nine o'clock, when Jonah checked his watch again, he knew Granville was absent.

Jonah's spirits sagged. How could he give Granville the trouble he deserved if Granville wouldn't show up to collect it? On top of everything else, it seemed that Granville Jones was lucky.

After handwriting, when Jonah finished only one row of capital *F*'s, Mrs. Lacey handed out stapled sheaves of paper to each child. Then she spent a long time explaining what they were to do with the papers.

Jonah listened to most of it. The papers were

part of the habitat study. There were questions you were supposed to answer about what animal you had chosen. And there were sentences with blanks you were supposed to fill in. There was construction paper on the art table for anyone who wanted to make a cover for his report. And there was a page in the report for drawing a picture of your animal.

Mrs. Lacey talked on. Like a radio that had slipped off the station, she began to sound like static to Jonah. *Buzz, buzz, buzz.* He stared at the papers.

Mrs. Lacey was saying something about Back-to-School Night. ". . . a week from tomorrow. So you'll have to work quickly."

Juliet's hand shot up. "Are we going to hang them up?" she asked.

"Yes," Mrs. Lacey said. "I've saved the other half of the bulletin board for the habitat reports."

Jonah turned to look at the bulletin board. He saw the empty half, and he saw the summer vacation reports on the other half. He could see his paragraph about the jet planes.

Uh-oh. That paragraph would still be hanging there on Back-to-School Night. His mother would see it. His *father* would see it. His father would think Jonah had lost his mind.

When it was time to start working, Jonah made a trip to the pencil sharpener. On the way back he detoured to the bulletin board and read his report. It was just as goofy as he remembered. Jonah shook his head.

Then he glanced at the paper hanging next to his. It was by Granville. "My Trip to the Moon," it was called. Jonah read it with growing amazement. In a full page and a half of his small, neat handwriting, Granville told about taking a summer vacation to the moon. "I had to go to the moon alone," it said. "In my old school I didn't have any friends. And my parents don't like space trips. And my sister is afraid. So I had to go all by myself. But it was real fun."

Jonah couldn't believe it. Why hadn't Mrs. Lacey made him do it over? It was obviously all made up. Nobody yet had ever taken a vacation to the moon.

Jonah returned to his seat feeling madder than ever at Granville. Granville could get away with anything. And even when he was absent, Granville found a way to make Jonah mad.

Jonah flipped to the first page of the habitat study. "My animal is a _____." Jonah wrote *hamster* in tiny letters.

"My animal weighs _____." Jonah got out the

hamster book and started leafing through the pages. He looked from front to back, then from back to front. Nowhere in the book did it say how much a hamster weighed. The author must have forgotten to weigh a hamster, Jonah figured. Or she couldn't weigh one. After all, it wasn't the kind of thing you could just weigh on a bathroom scale. In the blank space Jonah wrote: *Not much.*

He turned to the page of the habitat study that said: "Here Is a Picture of My Animal." Maybe he'd have better luck if he did the drawing first.

He drew the body, then the head and the nose. Then the eyes. The eyes were too beady, so Jonah erased them. He drew them again. They were too bulgy the next time.

This was tricky stuff. Jonah knew it would be easier if he were drawing a marmot. Or a jet plane. He was perfect at jets.

Jonah added two big wings to the hamster, tilted back. It reminded him of a fly. He added six legs and a proboscis, then two more wings. Then, using the side of his pencil, he colored in the body, black. A giant fly. It looked horrible. For some reason, it reminded Jonah of Granville.

Jonah drew a tag attached to the fly and wrote *Granville* on the tag. Next, up above, he drew a large flyswatter, with motion lines to show that it was coming down on the fly.

It was wonderful. Jonah laughed out loud. "Smash!" he said, and pounded the fly with his fist.

"Jonah," Mrs. Lacey said from behind him, "are you having any trouble?"

Jonah quickly spread his hands over the drawing. "No," he said. He could feel his cheeks getting hot.

"Do you want to show me what you're working on?"

Jonah hesitated. He wanted to say no, but somehow he knew it wouldn't work. Slowly he uncovered the drawing.

"I see . . ." Mrs. Lacey said. She stood and studied the drawing. Finally she said, "I'll tell you what, Jonah. Why don't you stop in and talk to me at lunch recess." Then she touched him lightly on the shoulder and moved away.

Jonah slumped forward and leaned his head on the desk. This was it. He had finally done it. Mrs. Lacey was disappointed in him. She knew he wasn't good enough for third grade. When she saw him at recess, she would be angry with him. Or, worse, she would just shake her head and give him The Look. The look that said: *You're a real disappointment, kid.*

Jonah couldn't bear it.

For the rest of the morning, and all through

lunch while Robbie chewed noisily on trail mix, Jonah couldn't think of anything except Mrs. Lacey and The Look.

He had rice cakes in his lunch. His mother had remembered that he liked rice cakes. He took a couple of bites; then he broke the rest into small pieces. His mother would be sorry she had remembered about the rice cakes when she got the note from Mrs. Lacey.

Jonah knew what the note would say. It would say: "Jonah doesn't do his work. He fiddles around. He doesn't pay attention. Jonah isn't ready for third-grade work." Something like that, Jonah thought.

His second-grade teacher had sent notes, and his first-grade teacher had sent notes. Even his kindergarten teacher had sent notes. And the notes had always made his mother mad. At Jonah.

"Hurry up," Robbie said. "Baseball today. We're playing outs."

"I might be late," Jonah said. Or I might not get there at all, he thought. Ever again. Second-graders didn't play with third-graders.

He drained his Thermos of milk and dumped the rest of his lunch in the garbage. Then he walked back to Room 4.

Mrs. Lacey was at her desk, dunking a tea bag

up and down in a mug of steaming water. Jonah walked up to her desk and stood there, waiting for her to notice him.

Mrs. Lacey stood and picked up her tea. "Let's sit over here," she said, going to one of the double student desks. Jonah slid into the seat next to her.

"Why don't you tell me about your habitat study," she said. She blew on her tea.

Jonah squirmed. "There's not much to tell," he said.

"What animal did you choose?"

"Hamster."

"Oh, a hamster. That's a perfectly good choice. What made you decide on a hamster?"

"I didn't," Jonah mumbled.

"Excuse me?"

"I didn't," Jonah repeated. "That is, I was looking at a hamster book, and I just picked it. It wasn't really my idea at all, if you know what I mean."

"No, I don't," Mrs. Lacey said. "Why don't you tell me what you mean."

Jonah took a deep breath. He wished he hadn't told her that the hamster wasn't his idea, but it was too late now.

"I was looking at it for Todd. Todd's my brother . . ."

"I know."

". . . and I thought he might want to know that hamsters don't eat people food, since he was feeding most of his dinners to Woz. Except dessert. I don't think he ever gave Woz a cookie. Only he wasn't. But I didn't know that. I just wanted to tell him so Woz wouldn't get sick. Woz is Todd's hamster."

Jonah stopped abruptly. He felt hopelessly tangled up. Mrs. Lacey had stopped blowing on her tea and was looking at him, holding the mug in her hands.

"What animal would you have chosen if you hadn't picked the hamster book? Accidentally, so to speak."

"A marmot," Jonah pronounced. That was easy.

"I see," Mrs. Lacey said. She resumed blowing on her tea. "And would you *like* doing a habitat study on marmots? Would you enjoy it?"

"Yeah," Jonah said. "I'd like it a lot. I know lots of stuff about marmots already. Like that they eat flowers and berries and things, and they whistle whenever there's danger. And they always have two or three entrances to their homes, and one entrance goes straight down for about two feet so the marmot can drop right in if he's scared. And they have nests in the den for keeping the babies after the grown-ups mate and the baby marmots are born."

Jonah stopped. He wasn't sure he should be talking to a teacher about mating and babies.

"Well, it sounds to me as if you know a great deal about marmots, Jonah. Maybe you'd like to do your habitat study on marmots. How would that be?"

"Great! Anyway, that's what I wanted to do all along."

"Fine. Then tomorrow I'll give you a new set of study papers," Mrs. Lacey said. Then she added, "And maybe this time you'll draw me a really terrific picture of a *marmot*."

"Yeah, I will," Jonah said.

Mrs. Lacey stood and carried her tea back to her desk. Jonah sat and watched her. Then he asked, "Are you going to write a note to my mother?"

"I shouldn't think so," Mrs. Lacey said. "Why, did you want me to?"

"No," Jonah said. "It's just that that's what teachers usually do when I forget to pay attention to my work. They write notes. And I take them home."

"Oh, I see. Well, tell me, Jonah—do you forget to pay attention to your work on purpose?"

"Of course not!" Jonah said. What a question!

"No . . . most children don't," Mrs. Lacey said. "You know, you're not the first child who ever had trouble paying attention. A lot of perfectly good adults were distractable children. My son was one of them. He's still absentminded. But he's a very good naval architect. And a thoroughly nice person."

Jonah stared. He was old enough to know that teachers didn't really live in the school. But he'd never thought of them having children. Grown-up children at that.

"Albert Einstein was another," Mrs. Lacey said. "Do you know who he was?"

"Sure!" Jonah said. Everyone knew about Einstein. He was a genius.

"His teachers thought he was hopeless," Mrs. Lacey laughed. "And even as an adult, he forgot simple things. Like socks. He couldn't remember to put on socks. But he was good at math."

"I wore my pajama top to school one day," Jonah confessed.

"And you're good at marmots," Mrs. Lacey said.

"So far. Maybe I'll be a marmot expert when I grow up," Jonah said.

"Maybe so. But right now you're still a third-grader. So why don't you go have recess with the other third-graders."

"Sure thing," Jonah said, and ran for the door.

The boys on the playing field were all either chasing each other around or were standing about in small groups, their hands in their pockets. Nobody was playing baseball.

"What's happening?" Jonah asked Robbie. "Why aren't we playing?"

"We quit," Robbie said.

"But why?"

"Because it's no fun without Granville. The only fielder we have who's halfway decent is Greg. Nobody can get any outs. It's boring."

Boring! It was wonderful. A recess without Granville was just what Jonah wanted most. But now, thanks to Granville, nobody wanted to play.

Granville was probably the only kid Jonah had ever met who could mess things up without even being there. Granville Jones was a royal pain!

ten

○ "MAYBE you should be the one to talk to Mr. Rosetti," Jonah said as his mother stood drying her hair on Wednesday morning.

"What? Jonah, I can't hear you." Mrs. Twist aimed the dryer at the top of her head.

"I said, maybe you should be the one to talk to Mr. Rosetti," Jonah yelled.

"What?" Jonah's mother switched off the dryer.

"I *said—*"

"No, I heard you. But I can't believe what I heard. You want *me* to talk to Mr. Rosetti?"

"Yeah. I just thought it might sound better if you explained things," Jonah said. "Sort of like people do in public relations. Dad says even the president of the United States has people who help him make things sound good." He sat on the edge of his mother's bed and thumped his lunch box against his knee.

"Jonah," his mother said, "there is no nice way of telling someone you flooded his yard, even if it was an accident. The best public relations firm in the world couldn't make that sound good."

"But . . ."

"The president of the United States couldn't make that sound good!"

"I didn't ask him," Jonah muttered.

"I mean it, Jonah. Mr. Rosetti won't be happy about it, but watering the yard was your job, and you're the one who flooded it. So you have to be the one who tells him."

Jonah bumped his lunch box from the left knee to the right. "But he wouldn't yell at you," he said.

"You're probably right," his mother said. "But the important thing is that responsible people admit their mistakes. And you have to be responsible enough to admit yours, young man."

"Aww, Mom . . ."

"Now hurry up," Mrs. Twist said, planting a kiss on his forehead. "You'll be late for school." She switched the dryer back on and started waving it at the side of her head.

"*Good-bye*," Jonah yelled at the top of his lungs.

That's the trouble with grown-ups, Jonah thought as he walked up Sonora Street—they think you can't do things you *can* do, and they think you can do things you *can't* do. And it was just like his mother to invent a new meaning for the word *responsible*, right when Jonah had gotten good at clearing his dishes.

Maybe Mr. Rosetti won't be home, Jonah thought. Maybe he's missed his plane and won't be back until later. Much later. January, for instance.

Jonah trudged up Mr. Rosetti's front steps, pushed the doorbell, and counted to ten. Nobody came.

Saved, Jonah thought, and bounded down the steps.

"Hello there, Jonah." Mr. Rosetti appeared from the driveway. He was holding a handful of radishes and wearing boots. "Were you looking for me?"

Jonah noticed that the boots were muddy.

"Mr. Rosetti I flooded your yard by mistake and it was an accident and it's okay if you don't pay me the pumpkin." There. He'd said it.

Mr. Rosetti walked to the front steps and sat down. "Well, it's soggy back there, all right," he said. "How did you do that, Jonah?"

"I went home for just a few minutes," Jonah said. "Only I forgot to come back." He sighed.

Mr. Rosetti shook some small clots of mud from the radishes. "My sister in Portland thinks I should move into an old people's home because I forgot where she keeps her silverware. I think I'll write to her and remind her that young boys forget things, too," he said.

"You could tell her Albert Einstein forgot his socks," Jonah offered.

Mr. Rosetti laughed.

"I think your tomatoes are ruined, though," Jonah went on. "My dad says they'll probably burst."

"Oh, yes. Some already have. But I was going to use most of them for canning my homemade tomato sauce anyway. 'Rosetti's Supreme Tomato Sauce,' I call it. I imagine it'll taste every bit as good with burst tomatoes as with whole ones, don't you?"

"I guess so," Jonah said. Then he thought a minute. "But I'm still sorry," he said.

"I appreciate that, Jonah," Mr. Rosetti said, standing up. "And I'll still expect you to come collect that pumpkin, okay?"

"I can? I mean, you will?"

"Of course. After all, I asked you to water my garden, and you certainly watered it."

Jonah laughed. "I sure did," he said. He wanted to hug Mr. Rosetti, but he stuck out his hand instead. "Thanks, Mr. Rosetti."

Mr. Rosetti grasped Jonah's hand with his own muddy one. "My pleasure, Jonah," he said.

Jonah jogged the rest of the way to Mills Elementary School. As he came in sight of the school grounds, he could see they were empty. He knew he was late. And he didn't care. He had the feeling that Mrs. Lacey wasn't going to get mad at him just for being a little late once in a while. He had the feeling Mrs. Lacey was his friend.

He knew one thing for sure—she didn't think he was hopeless. Albert Einstein should have had Mrs. Lacey, Jonah thought.

He stood outside the door to Room 4 until he could hear the end of the Pledge of Allegiance; then he went inside.

"You're tardy," Juliet said. "Jonah's tardy, Mrs. Lacey."

Mrs. Lacey picked up a piece of chalk and began writing math problems on the board. She acted as if she hadn't heard Juliet.

Jonah plopped into his seat.

"You're late," Granville said.

"Big wow," Jonah said.

"I was absent yesterday," Granville said. "I went to the dentist and he had to gas me. See?" He opened his mouth and pointed to a shiny new filling on a back tooth.

Jonah pulled out a blank piece of binder paper and his pencil. He didn't answer Granville.

"Then I got this," Granville said. He held up his arm, displaying a black leather wristband with chrome studs.

Jonah started copying down the first math problem from the board. Granville shrugged.

At the end of math time Granville had finished all ten problems. Jonah had worked hard. His hardest ever. He'd finished seven. He wrote his name, half cursive, half printing, in large letters at the top of the page. Then he passed it forward.

Mrs. Lacey told everyone to get out their habitat studies to work on. She walked up to Jonah and handed him his new sheaf of study papers. Then she gave some to Granville.

"Jonah will explain what to do with these," she said to Granville.

"Oh, but . . ." Jonah said.

"You'll do fine, Jonah," Mrs. Lacey said.

Jonah looked at Granville and took a deep breath. "You're supposed to fill in all the blanks," he said. "If you don't know the answer, look it up in your book."

"That's it?" Granville asked. "I could have figured that out for myself."

Jonah picked up his pencil. In the space where

it said: "My animal is a _____," Jonah wrote *marmot*. Then he filled in the space about weight. *12 pounds*, he wrote. Then in parentheses he wrote (*less in winter*).

"How do you spell *chameleon*?" Granville asked.

"Beats me," Jonah said. He turned to a page headed: "Other Interesting Facts About My Animal." He started writing.

A marmot is a rodent. Which is exactly what a rat is. But marmots are much cuter than rats. They're more like a big, fat squirrel that lives under ground. And they are the most like a groundhog. If you want to see a marmot you should go camping in the Sierra Nevada. And you can feed them if you want because they are very friendly. But you *should not* feed them because it is not healthy for them. This summer I told nine people to stop feeding the marmots. One man was from Denmark and he did not speak English. But he understood.

He had filled the whole page, and the work period wasn't even over yet. Jonah couldn't believe it.

"I might get a mohawk," Granville said. "Then I'll look really awesome."

Jonah groaned. Granville didn't *need* to look more awesome, he thought. What Granville needed was to sit someplace else.

Jonah remembered his plan. He reached his hand in his desk and felt around. His fingers closed on the packet of gum. He pulled it out and peeled the top off.

"Want some gum?" he asked Granville.

"Naw," Granville said.

"It's bubble gum."

"Does it have sugar?" Granville asked.

"Sure," Jonah said. "It's delicious."

"No way, then. I just had a filling." He stuck a finger in his mouth. "My mother will kill me if I get another cavity."

"You don't get cavities in just one day. Come on."

"Mrs. Lacey will get mad."

"No, she won't," Jonah lied.

Granville looked suspicious. "Are you trying to get me in trouble?"

Jonah began to feel nervous. This was harder than he'd thought it would be.

"Of course not," Jonah said. "Can't you tell when someone's trying to be your friend?"

"You want to be my friend?" Granville looked astonished.

"Sure," Jonah lied firmly.

"Well, then . . ." Granville reached over and took a piece of gum. Jonah watched as the wrapper fell to the floor.

"Good," Granville chewed.

"Have another," Jonah offered.

Granville took another.

"Have as many as you like," Jonah said. "Have them all."

Granville took several more. Jonah watched as the space around Granville's chair became littered with wrappers.

"This is great gum," Granville said. "Thanks. Do you *really* want to be my friend?"

Jonah gulped. "Sure," he said again.

"Awesome," Granville said. He chewed harder.

"Try a bubble," Jonah nudged.

"I don't think it's ready yet."

"Try. Just try."

Granville worked the gum around his mouth. Then he started a small bubble. It fizzled.

"Granville Jones," Mrs. Lacey said, "are you actually chewing gum in my class?"

"Yeah." Granville beamed.

This is it, Jonah thought gleefully.

"Whatever possessed you?" Mrs. Lacey said to Granville. "And there are wrappers all over the floor!"

"Jonah gave it to me," Granville said. "He's my best friend." He slung an arm over Jonah's shoulder.

98

Jonah buried his face in his hands. The trap was supposed to be for *Granville,* not for Jonah. He hadn't counted on this.

"I see," Mrs. Lacey said. "Well, I'm very pleased that you're such good friends. But I would appreciate it if you'd keep the gum part of your friendship *out*side of class."

"Sure thing," Granville said. He picked up an empty wrapper and spit the wad of gum into it. "Sorry, Jonah," he said.

Sorry? *He* was sorry? Jonah was frantic. Granville was the fastest, toughest, smartest, and luckiest kid Jonah had ever met. You can't even get him in trouble for something that *everyone* gets busted for, Jonah thought.

And now Mrs. Lacey would never move Jonah's seat. Granville thought Jonah was his best friend, and so did Mrs. Lacey. It was amazing. It was *ridiculous.* It was the dumbest thing Jonah had ever heard.

Unexpectedly, Jonah started to laugh. He tried to stop, but the harder he tried, the harder he laughed. He laughed so hard tears rolled down his cheeks and he started to hiccup. Granville thumped him on the back, but Jonah couldn't stop laughing. Mrs. Lacey sent him to the boys' room to calm down.

Jonah, best friends with Granville Jones? Who had ever heard of anything so silly?

○ For the rest of the day, Granville followed Jonah everywhere. He sat next to Jonah at lunch. And at lunch recess, when Granville was chosen captain of the team, he picked Jonah first.

When it was his turn to pick, Jonah picked Robbie.

"Hey," Robbie said. "It's great that Granville's your best friend, because now we can always have him on our team."

"It's not great," Jonah said. "It's dumb. It's an accident. Besides, it's just temporary."

After school, Granville was waiting for Jonah outside the front door. Jonah walked past him, but Granville caught up and fell into step beside Jonah.

"Do you want to come over to my house?" Granville asked.

"No," Jonah said.

"How 'bout tomorrow, then?"

"*No*," Jonah said.

"How 'bout the next day, then?"

"*NO*," Jonah yelled.

"Why not?" Granville asked. "I thought you wanted to be my friend."

"Forget it," Jonah said. "That was a mistake. I don't want to be friends with you."

"But *why*?" Granville persisted.

"Because. Because I wouldn't be friends with someone who jumps out from behind bushes all the time."

"I won't do that anymore," Granville said. "I didn't do it today, did I?"

"Or jumps out of trees," Jonah said. "I hate it when you jump out of trees and scream."

"I won't do that anymore, either. Promise."

"But you want to kill me. You said so. You said you could kill me with your bare hands."

"I made that up," Granville said. "I wouldn't really kill you. I *couldn't* kill you. I don't know anything about karate or any of that stuff."

Jonah stopped walking. "But you *said* . . ."

"I made it all up," Granville repeated. "When you're the littlest person in the state, you have to act tough. Or they'll pulverize you. But I couldn't kill you even if I wanted to. I don't know how."

"Honest?" Jonah stared at Granville. Was he really just an ordinary, everyday short person?

"Honest. Promise you won't tell anyone, though. Until I grow, that is."

"Well . . ." Jonah hesitated.

"So you'll come over?" Granville asked.

"I don't know. . . ."

"Come on," Granville said. "I'll let you play with my best Transformer."

Jonah walked on in silence, thinking. It was a lot to get used to—the idea that Granville wasn't really some kind of miniature terrorist. And that he wanted to be Jonah's friend. Was it possible that Jonah had made a mistake about Granville? Had Mrs. Lacey been right all along?

"My mother bakes great cookies," Granville said. "She bakes all the time. She's kind of fat, but she thinks if I eat lots of cookies I'll grow. She'll give some to you."

"Maybe . . ." Jonah said.

"And if you come spend the night, she'll bake a whole cake. Two, maybe."

Jonah laughed. "I couldn't eat a whole cake," he said.

"So you'll come?" Granville asked.

"Maybe," Jonah said. Then he thought. "On one condition," he said. "If I come to spend the night, you have to show me how you glow in the dark."

"Dummy," Granville said. "*No*body glows in the dark."

eleven

o ON THURSDAY evening of the next week, Jonah stood in the kitchen and watched as his mother packed his lunch for the next day. He wished she'd hurry up. Jonah was going to spend the night at Granville's house while their parents went to Back-to-School Night. He was anxious to leave.

Todd had protested. He said *he'd* never been allowed to have an overnight on a school night, so why should Jonah. But Mrs. Twist just said, "I think Jonah can handle it," and that was that.

"You'll tell Dad about my vacation report, won't you?" Jonah asked.

"That you made it up?" Mrs. Twist asked. "Yes, I'll tell him, Jonah."

"And that it was *okay* to make things up," Jonah said. "Granville made his up, too, and it's even more made up than mine is, if you know what I mean."

Mrs. Twist laughed. "No, I don't," she said. "But knowing Granville, anything's possible." She snapped the lid shut on Jonah's lunch box and handed it to him.

"Thanks," Jonah said. "See you later."

"Hold it," Mrs. Twist said. "Haven't you forgotten something?"

"A hug," Jonah said, and delivered one.

"And don't forget to brush your teeth. And don't dawdle in the morning. And don't forget to say thank-you. And don't forget . . ." She hesitated.

"My brain?" Jonah supplied.

"No." Mrs. Twist reached out and tousled his hair. "To have fun."

"I won't," Jonah said. "I always have fun with Granville."

As he walked down Sonora Street in the gathering dusk, Jonah realized that that was true. He always did have fun with Granville. Ever since they had become friends, that is—which had been for a whole week. It seemed like forever to Jonah. It was hard for him to remember when he hadn't liked Granville.

And Granville was more than fun. He was useful.

Like last Monday in school.

Jonah had been working on his spelling sentences when he got stuck on the word *great*. He couldn't remember if that was the kind that meant terrific, or the kind that his mother did with cheese. So Jonah sat staring into space for a long time, trying to think of a sentence that would be right for both words.

People around him were finishing already and passing in their papers. Jonah began to get that familiar sinking feeling. Today he wouldn't be just slow. He would be last. Again.

Then he heard Juliet's voice, more piercing than usual. "Jonah isn't done, Mrs. Lacey. He isn't even *working*."

Jonah started to slide down in his seat. People were turning to look at him.

Just then, Granville shoved his chair back and stood up. Then he climbed onto his chair and turned toward Juliet. When he spoke, it was in a voice even louder and more piercing than Juliet's had been.

"*Juliet Nosy Fisher,*" he said. "*Mind your own business.*" Then he climbed down and turned to Mrs. Lacey. "Excuse me," he mumbled, and sat back down.

Jonah was amazed. He sat frozen for a minute, waiting for Juliet to cry or make an announcement about Granville. Or for Mrs. Lacey to tell Granville she wanted to see him at recess. But nobody said anything. Juliet just sat there with her mouth clamped shut and her cheeks red. And Jonah thought he saw a little smile on one side of Mrs. Lacey's face.

Then Jonah remembered. He bent over his paper and wrote:

Juliet isn't so <u>great</u>.

He shoved it over in front of Granville and Granville laughed. Juliet hadn't made another announcement since.

○ And like on Tuesday afternoon when Jonah and Granville were building a lunar colony out of their combined Space Lego on the floor of Granville's room. Granville's cat walked in and sat right down in the middle of the shuttle launchpad.

"That's the fattest cat I ever saw in my life," Jonah said, petting it. He wondered if Granville's mother fed it cookies, too. Mrs. Jones's cookies were everything Granville had promised, and more.

"That's Mulberry," Granville said. "She's pregnant. She's supposed to have her kittens next week. Mom thinks she'll have six."

"Wow," Jonah said. "You're lucky. I want a cat, but I don't know if I can get one yet."

"You can have one of these kittens," Granville offered. "I'll even let you pick your favorite. But you'll have to wait a while before you can take it home."

"Great!" Jonah said. Then he stopped himself. "The thing is, I don't know if I can have a pet anytime soon. I have to wait until I'm very responsible, and I don't know how long that's going to take."

"Being responsible is hard," Granville said.

"You're telling me," Jonah said.

"And it's not one of the things you're naturally good at."

"I know," Jonah said.

Granville worked on a laser intercept system for one of the spaceships for a while. Then he said, "You may have to find another way."

"Probably," Jonah sighed. "But what?"

"Like when the kitten is big enough you take it to your house and show it to your mother. She'll think it's so cute she'll let you keep it. That's how I got this cat."

Jonah thought about this. He thought that maybe the kind of mother who baked cookies was the same kind of mother who would think a kitten was cute. But Jonah's mother didn't bake cookies.

"I don't know," Jonah said. "My mother's tough."

"But is she tough *enough?*" Granville said. "Kittens are *really* cute."

"True," Jonah said, his hopes rising. At least it was worth a try. It was better than waiting to become responsible.

○ "I've been waiting for you forever," Granville said from the doorway of his house. It was a warm evening, and Granville was wearing a white T-shirt with the sleeves rolled up and a pair of shorts with stripes down the sides.

Jonah stretched his legs to take the front steps two at a time, even though he was weighed down with his lunch box, binder, duffel, and sleeping bag.

"Sorry," Jonah said. "I got here as fast as I could."

"In my room, quick," Granville said, leading the way down the hall. "I've got something to show you. It's awesome. It's radical. It's *so cool.*"

As they passed by the linen closet, Jonah stopped. The door was open just a few inches. Jonah opened it wider. He knew what was in there. The day before, on some rags in the bottom of the closet, Mulberry had had her kittens. Six of them. Jonah had arrived in time to see the last two being born. He reached in and lightly stroked the back of the smallest kitten. Its fur was a reddish brown, and it was the kitten Jonah liked best. It reminded him of a marmot.

"Hurry," Granville urged from the door of his room.

"Coming," Jonah said.

He dropped his things on the floor of Granville's room and stood looking at the wall where Granville gestured with an open hand.

An oversized poster hung on the wall. It was a poster of Sylvester Stallone. As Rocky.

"What do you think?" Granville asked, grinning.

"Awesome," Jonah said.

"See the resemblance?" Granville asked.

"Uh . . ."

"To *me,*" Granville said.

"Oh. Well . . ." Jonah stared at the poster. He didn't see any resemblance. In fact, if there was one person in the world who Granville didn't look like in any way, it was Rocky. Jonah wondered if Granville's feelings would be hurt if he told him so.

"Of course, I'm not grown up yet," Granville said.

"Well, no. But . . ."

"And of course his face is different," Granville added.

"Yeah, but . . ."

"But except for that, I'm just like him, right?"

"Well . . ." Jonah said. He tried to think of a way to say no that didn't sound like no.

"We're exactly alike," Granville said.

"Gee, Granville. I don't . . ."

"On the *in*side, you wookie. I'm just like him on the *in*side."

"*Oh*," Jonah said, relieved. "Now I see. Yeah, I guess you are alike in a way."

"In lots of ways," Granville corrected.

"Yeah," Jonah said.

Granville struck a Rocky pose in front of the poster. "I'm invincible, see?"

Jonah laughed. "Yeah. And sort of weird, too."

"*Very* weird," Granville laughed, jabbing at Jonah. "And *big*." He stood on his tiptoes.

"*Very* big," Jonah agreed. "A giant."